# THE
# ROCKING
# CHAIR
# PROPHET

## MATTHEW KELLY

**BLUE** sparrow

## THE ROCKING CHAIR PROPHET

Copyright © 2023 Kakadu, LLC
Published by Blue Sparrow
An Imprint of Viident

All rights reserved.
No part of this book may be used or reproduced in any manner whatsoever without permission except in the case of brief quotations in critical articles or reviews.

This is a work of fiction. Any names or characters, businesses or places, events or incidents, are fictitious. Any resemblance to actual persons, living or dead, or actual events is purely coincidental.

ISBN: 978-1-63582-208-3 (hardcover)
ISBN: 978-1-63582-209-0 (eBook)

*Design by*
Ashley Dias and Matthew Kelly

To learn more, visit:
TheRockingChairProphet.com

10 9 8 7 6 5 4 3 2

FIRST EDITION

Printed in the United States of America

# TABLE OF CONTENTS

EPIGRAPH — VI

1. EMPTY ROOMS — 1
2. SLEEPLESS NIGHT — 6
3. CROWDED HOUSE — 9
4. THE FUNERAL — 11
5. WHEN NOTHING MAKES SENSE — 13
6. SAY GOODBYE TO IT ALL — 16
7. THE LETTER — 17
8. THE LAST SIGHTING — 19
9. DISAPPEARED — 19
10. OLD FRIENDS — 19
11. THE CAVEMAN — 20
12. THE EVENING NEWS — 20
13. THE HERMIT — 22
14. DO YOU THINK IT'S HIM? — 25
15. HEALING AND HYSTERIA — 28
16. THE WORLD BEATS A PATH — 32
17. AN INSTINCT TO RETURN — 32
18. HOMECOMING — 35
19. EZRA'S DREAM — 37
20. CRAZY OLD MAN — 40
21. ASKING FOR HELP — 42
22. MIDLIFE CRISIS — 46
23. THE EXTRAORDINARY ORDINARY — 49

| | | |
|---|---|---|
| 24. | AWARENESS | 53 |
| 25. | SUNDAY MORNING | 55 |
| 26. | ONE MAN'S TRASH | 56 |
| 27. | THE BRUTAL TRUTH | 59 |
| 28. | LOVE | 64 |
| 29. | QUESTIONS | 70 |
| 30. | THE CHILL OF DESTINY | 75 |
| 31. | LOVE REKINDLED | 76 |
| 32. | WORSHIPPING EFFICIENCY | 78 |
| 33. | A FATHER'S CONCERN | 81 |
| 34. | OLD SELF AND NEW SELF | 81 |
| 35. | DEEPLY PERSONAL QUESTIONS | 82 |
| 36. | AMBITION'S PRISONER | 84 |
| 37. | THE ANSWERS ARE WITHIN | 88 |
| 38. | NOBLE SERVICE | 93 |
| 39. | MAKING PREPARATIONS | 95 |
| 40. | DEPRESSION | 97 |
| 41. | EZRA'S GRATITUDE | 100 |
| 42. | ANTICIPATION | 102 |
| 43. | SLEEPLESS NIGHT | 102 |
| 44. | A MIDSUMMER NIGHT | 104 |
| 45. | THE MEANING OF LIFE | 106 |
| 46. | THE GOD QUESTION | 108 |
| 47. | GRATITUDE | 110 |
| 48. | THE CRITIC | 113 |
| 49. | A HEAVY MOOD | 120 |
| 50. | HEALTH | 121 |
| 51. | THE GOOD LIFE | 123 |
| 52. | PARENTS AND CHILDREN | 124 |

| | |
|---|---|
| 53. MONEY AND THINGS | 125 |
| 54. SPIRITUALITY | 127 |
| 55. GENEROSITY | 129 |
| 56. WORK | 131 |
| 57. LEARNING | 133 |
| 58. NATURE | 134 |
| 59. THANK YOU | 136 |
| 60. BLISSFUL EXUBERANCE | 137 |
| 61. A PROUD FATHER | 138 |
| 62. THE MORNING AFTER | 140 |
| 63. YOUR DREAMS KNOW THE WAY | 142 |
| 64. EXHAUSTION | 144 |
| 65. EVERYONE'S CURIOUS | 145 |
| 66. A NEW YEARNING | 147 |
| 67. RESTLESS | 148 |
| 68. THE NOTE | 151 |
| 69. A SEASON FOR EVERYTHING | 153 |

*"Behold,
I am doing something new!
Now it springs forth."*

Isaiah 43:19

# 1. EMPTY ROOMS

You never really know who you are until you have suffered. Really suffered. But once you know, you can never forget, and from that moment on things you never considered become possible.

Daniel had never suffered. Not really. Like us all, he'd had his share of heartaches and disappointments. But he had never experienced the crucible of suffering that strips away everything that is superfluous and redefines what makes life worth living.

You thought you knew Daniel the moment you saw him. He reminded everyone of someone from their past. He was one of those people who made everything look easy. Gifted beyond belief, effortlessly good-looking, and with the whole world at his feet, Daniel was confident but never arrogant. And the instant you thought you knew him, he would surprise you with uncommon thoughtfulness. It was unexpected because people expected him to be self-absorbed.

It was Friday afternoon. The valet casually tossed Daniel's keys through the air, and he palmed them with ease. Settling into his Maserati, he turned the key in the ignition, and the car roared to life.

Daniel loved cars. It seemed everyone on Wall Street did. He worked in an industry well known for an insatiable appetite for cars, watches, women, and homes. But this was another way Daniel defied the stereotypes. He had one car, one watch, one woman, and one home.

If Daniel had one fault, it was going with the flow. That's how he ended up on Wall Street. All men's lives have ambiguities and inconsistencies. This was his. It was the one piece of his life that just didn't seem to make sense.

The drive home didn't bother him. The end-of-week traffic was insane, with everyone trying to escape the city. But he cherished these days when he drove to and from work, and little by little, as he made his way toward home, the traffic fell away.

Daniel enjoyed the drive. It gave him time to decompress. It gave him time to call his parents. And it gave him time to listen to music, and few people appreciated music more than Daniel.

It was summer, and he was looking forward to spending the weekend with his girls. He had an amazing wife, Jessica, and they had two daughters—Julia, who was almost nine, and Jordan, who was seven. They reminded Daniel of all the good things life had to offer. And they often pointed out that he was working too much and missing out on hiking in the mountains, picking wild strawberries, and watching soul-shifting sunsets.

"You only get 365 sunsets a year, Dad," Julia would say.

"Yeah, and I'm gonna be going off to college in about five minutes," Jordan would tease.

Daniel was a practical guy with a wonderful sense of humor, so he would smile and say, "I know. And I'm working hard to make sure you don't have any of those nasty student loans that plague so many people's lives!"

Driving home that night, he was also driving toward his thirty-third birthday. It wasn't until tomorrow, but he knew the festivities would begin as soon as he walked through the door.

He had never been one to get caught up in birthdays, but thirty-three had him thinking that he was creeping toward what his friends called "halftime." And that had put him in a more reflective mood than usual this year as his birthday approached.

As he pulled into the driveway, a sudden chill went through him. He sensed something wasn't right, but he pushed that thought aside. The sun hadn't set, but the house seemed dark and still. It looked eerily quiet, and Daniel wondered how a house could look quiet.

*Surprise party*, he thought and smiled.

He took the steps leading up to the front door two at a time and turned the doorknob. It was locked. *Weird,* he thought. Fumbling for his keys, he couldn't remember the last time the door had been locked when he got home. But he pushed that thought aside too, suspecting it was a tactic to let everyone get in position for the surprise.

Stepping inside the front door, he paused to give everyone a chance to jump out and scream, "Surprise!" But they didn't. The house was empty.

His suit jacket was flung over the watch on his left wrist, just above his briefcase. It was a navy soft-sided leather bag his wife had given him last Christmas.

Daniel reached for the light switch with his right hand as he called out, "I'm home." But there was no response. "Jessica! Julia! Jordan?" he called, but still no reply. He started wondering what he might have forgotten. School play? No, it was the middle of summer. Sport? No, it was that brief time of year when the girls were between sports.

The panic that perhaps he had forgotten something quickly subsided as he recalled the last thing his wife had said to him on the phone earlier that day: "A whole weekend of nothing. No plans, no commitments, nothing to do but celebrate the man we love."

"Where are they?" he mused.

Daniel didn't like wondering, so he picked up his phone and dialed Jessica. It didn't ring. It went straight to voicemail. *That's strange*, he thought and dialed again. But the same thing happened.

He grabbed an ice-cold bottle of Coke from the refrigerator, turned on some lights, and headed out onto the front porch to wait for his girls to come home.

It was a magnificent evening. The colors in the sky were captivating. Daniel could hear children playing ball, an occasional dog barking, and the cheerful conversation of neighbors a couple of doors down. Sitting on the top step, he continued to wonder where his girls were. Perhaps they had gone to buy him a last-minute gift in town.

At that moment, Mrs. Turnbull walked by with her three Corgis. They always made Daniel think of the Queen of England. Pleasantries were exchanged, but she didn't stop. She kept moving purposefully toward the park at the end of the street.

The sun was starting to set now. It would be dark in forty-five minutes, and Daniel was starting to worry. He looked at his watch again. He had been sitting on the steps for almost an hour. It felt like four.

As the final moments of dusk were lingering, bidding farewell to the day, Daniel heard a car coming down the street. *About time*, he thought and told himself not to get into an argument about why his wife had turned off her phone.

That thought died when he watched in disbelief as a police cruiser pulled into his driveway. Two officers stepped out of the car and began to walk toward him. Daniel froze. His heart seized up. He couldn't breathe. He wanted to vomit. Tears started streaming down his face.

He knew. In some inexplicable way, he had sensed it the moment he pulled into his driveway.

"Daniel, I'm Chief Rigger, and I believe you know Sergeant Thompson." Daniel could see the officer's lips moving, but he couldn't hear anything he was saying. There was a ringing in his ears, and he felt numb allover. "Do you mind if we come inside?" Chief Rigger continued. But Daniel couldn't move. It was as if he were cast in stone. "Daniel?"

Daniel tried to speak, but no words came out. Sergeant Thompson took him by the arm, helped him up, walked him into the living room, and settled him in the big armchair where Daniel liked to sit and watch football.

"Daniel, I can tell by your reaction that you know something horrible has happened." Daniel stared at him and through him. "We regret to inform you that your wife Jessica, and your two daughters, Julia and Jordan, were all killed in a car accident earlier this evening."

The tears that had stopped began to stream down Daniel's cheeks again. *This can't be happening. There must be some kind of mistake*, he thought. "Are you sure it was them?" he asked, grasping hopelessly.

"We are sure. I'm sorry, Daniel," the police chief said with an empathy that was practiced, and yet sincere.

"What happened?" Daniel stammered.

"It seems five or six deer came out in front of a truck. The truck hit the deer, throwing them onto the other side of the road. Your wife was driving in the other direction and struck the deer, causing her vehicle to spin out of control. Her car crossed the median and was struck by another truck."

"Where?"

"Out on Route 12, about a mile from Johnson's Farm Store," Sergeant Thompson offered.

"The trucker?" Daniel mumbled.

"He has been hospitalized. He has no physical injuries, but he's literally out of his mind with anguish. He had to be sedated at the scene, and they will keep him sedated for at least twenty-four hours."

"It wasn't his fault?" Daniel asked.

The police chief spoke again now, choosing his words carefully, "No. It wasn't his fault. It wasn't anyone's fault. Our analyst has been at the scene for hours, and she has concluded it was a dreadful accident."

"I wonder what they were doing out that way this afternoon?" Daniel asked himself out loud.

"It seems they had bought a whole bunch of peaches at Johnson's Farm Store," the chief said.

"Ah . . . Jessica was probably going to make my peach cobbler. Her peach cobbler is not of this world," Daniel muttered. And then lifting his eyes to a faraway place he said, "My peach cobbler killed my gorgeous girls."

"Be careful now, Daniel," Sergeant Thompson said, "that's a dangerous path to start down."

"You're right. Yes, you're right. I just . . ." Daniel said unconsciously.

Wiping his tears away, Daniel stood up. He thanked the officers for coming and walked them to the door, as if he were concluding a routine meeting at the office. It was a reflexive action brought on by shock and the early stages of grief.

## 2. SLEEPLESS NIGHT

Daniel didn't sleep that night.

As soon as he closed the front door, he walked over to the freezer, pulled out an unopened bottle of vodka, reached into the kitchen cabinet for the biggest glass he could find, and filled it with the cool, clear liquid. When he finished, he poured himself another, and then another. When the bottle was empty, he started in on the rum.

Daniel wandered aimlessly around the house, moving from room to room. The air was thick with memories. He remembered saying goodbye that very morning. He tried to engrave those last hugs, that last kiss, those last moments in his mind. Daniel was overwhelmed with a fear that he would forget them. Those last hugs reminded him that when he held his girls, the sweet smell of their hair drifted through the air.

Now, he stumbled toward his bedroom, grabbed the pillow from his wife's side of the bed, and buried his face in it. There it was, the smell of her face, the smell of her hair. Crying into Jessica's pillow, he wanted to hold on to that smell forever.

Daniel sat there with the pillow for a long time. When he finally got up, he went into Julia's room, grabbed her pillow, and did the same thing. *She will never go to college*, he thought to himself. *She will never get to see the world. She will never get to pursue her talents or chase her dreams. I will never walk her down the aisle. She will never have children. I'll never get to meet my grandchildren.*

After about twenty minutes, he went into Jordan's room and did the same thing. "My baby, my poor baby girl," he wept into the pillow, smelling her hair and her soft skin.

His grief was paralyzing. He wandered around the house for hours, bumping into memories and broken dreams. This was eventually interrupted by a knock on the door. He wasn't sure what time it was. Daniel stumbled toward the front door. It was Jessica's parents, Mitch and Amanda Ferguson.

"Sorry to knock so loud, son," Mitch apologized. "We've been ringing the doorbell for about ten minutes."

Daniel squinted at his in-laws. The sun was up. "What time is it?" Daniel asked, slurring his words and searching for something to say.

"Eight o'clock, son," Mitch replied gently. "Can we come in?"

"Sure, yes . . . sorry," Daniel said as he stumbled out of the way, realizing he was blocking the doorway. "How did you get here so fast?" he continued, very drunk and at a loss for what to say.

"We drove all night," Amanda spoke now. "We tried to call, but there was no answer."

Daniel looked around for his phone and seeing it on the kitchen counter, staggered toward it. "Seventy-four missed calls," he said, again speaking to himself.

Mitch, Amanda, and Daniel stood in the middle of the living room. They glanced at each other before casting their gaze toward the floor. Three people desperately in need of consolation, but it was in short supply. Three starving people hoping the others had a crust of bread.

"You been drinking?" Mitch asked.

"Yep," Daniel replied. "Would you like one?"

"Yeah, I think I would. Can I help myself?" Daniel waved him in the direction of the liquor.

"Have you slept?" Amanda asked. Daniel glared at her in a way that made it clear that he had not. "Would you like to lie down for a couple of hours?" she persisted, but he didn't reply.

Amanda went into the bathroom, and both Mitch and Daniel could hear that she was on the phone, but not what she was saying.

Fifteen minutes later the doorbell rang again. Daniel, in a daze, didn't move, so Amanda got up and answered the door. It was Javier, Daniel's best friend since childhood.

Javier sat down next to Daniel. "I'm not gonna ask how you are or pretend that this isn't a brutal situation. I'm here for two reasons. First, because I'm your friend. Second, to help you get some sleep, because as a doctor, I know sleep is what you need right now."

"I don't want to sleep," Daniel said firmly.

"I know, man, but you also don't know what you want to do, or what you should do, or anything else right now. This might be the first time in your entire life that you don't know," Javier explained calmly.

Daniel didn't smile. Javier didn't expect him to, but he could see that his point had registered, despite the massive amount of alcohol Daniel had consumed.

"I brought something to help you sleep. So, there are two ways this can play out. I can wrestle you to the ground like in high school or you can walk down the hall, get out of that suit, lie down, and let me give you the shot so you can drift into a deep sleep."

Daniel didn't speak. He didn't move. He didn't look at Javier. He gazed off into the empty distance. Javier sat patiently, allowing the moment to unfold, waiting for his friend's response.

Two minutes later, Daniel got up and walked down the hallway. Javier followed.

"Nobody goes into any of the bedrooms," Daniel barked. "Nobody!"

Ten minutes later he was fast asleep in the guest room.

## 3. CROWDED HOUSE

Daniel woke twelve hours later. He was dreaming he was lying on the sidewalk in a puddle of rain. Javier was sitting exactly where he had been when Daniel fell asleep. "What time is it?"

"About nine," Javier replied.

"It sounds like there are a hundred people in the house," Daniel said.

"Yep. Your parents made it back from their trip to California, and there are a lot of people who want to be here for you. They started showing up around ten o'clock this morning."

The wet sensation Daniel had been dreaming about turned out not to have been a dream. "Did I wet the bed?" he asked Javier.

"Yeah, I'm pretty sure you did. All that alcohol had to go somewhere," Javier mused. "Do you want me to ask everyone to leave?"

"No, that's okay."

"I put a fresh set of clothes in the bathroom for you."

Daniel got out of bed dazed and groggy, went into the bathroom, and turned on the shower. Javier went to the living room and let Daniel's parents know that he was awake and would be out soon.

Twenty minutes later, Daniel's parents made their way down the hallway. They met their broken son as he came out of the bathroom, and both hugged him at the same time. He melted into the love of their embrace, and all three wept. Neither Daniel nor his parents said anything. They all knew words were woefully inadequate amid such soul-crushing tragedy.

After the longest embrace of his life, Daniel made his way toward the living room, where he was greeted by a sea of family and friends that overflowed into the front yard and the backyard. He didn't make it into the crowd. They started approaching him as soon as they saw him.

Few words were spoken. Those that were, Daniel didn't hear. He had retreated into the traumatized daze Javier had found him in that morning. And there was a buzzing in his head. People hugged him, shook hands, and offered help, but he knew nobody could help him now. Not yet. *Maybe in a few weeks, or months . . . but maybe never*, he thought to himself.

It was almost midnight by the time everyone left.

"I wish you would let us stay here with you," his mother said. "But we will respect your desire to be alone." She desperately wanted to stay with her son, but he had made it clear he wanted to be alone. Holding back tears, she continued, "We're all staying at the inn. If you need anything, we can be here in five minutes. Call at any hour. I left the phone number and our room number on the refrigerator."

Daniel turned instinctively to look at the refrigerator. It was covered with photos. His wife and daughters were smiling at him. It felt like someone had stabbed him in the heart. Feeling light-headed, he dropped to his knees and began to weep again. His mother immediately realized her mistake. She got down on the ground, wrapped Daniel in her arms, and held him tight.

After his parents had left, Javier said, "I'd like to give you something to get you back to sleep." Daniel had no fight left in him. He walked back to the guest room, undressed down to his boxers and T-shirt, and got into bed. He had been wounded to the core, shattered into a thousand pieces.

"Happy birthday!" Daniel said sarcastically to himself as he felt the sedative taking effect.

## 4. THE FUNERAL

The days that followed were a blur. Before he knew it, Daniel was sitting in the front pew at church staring at three white coffins. *My girls, my girls, my beautiful girls* . . . was all he kept thinking.

The Pastor was speaking, but Daniel couldn't hear. He didn't want to hear. He wasn't interested in words.

Getting up in the middle of the Pastor's remarks, Daniel began walking around the coffins, circling them in silence. When he came to the head of his wife's, he stopped, casting his eyes back and forth between it and the two smaller coffins on either side.

The Pastor stopped speaking.

Now, for the first time in almost a week, Daniel spoke. It was as if nobody else was there, just Daniel and the three coffins in a big, old, empty church.

Placing his right hand on his wife's coffin, he murmured, "My wonderful wife, what a blessing you were to me. Thank you for loving me, Jessica, even when I didn't deserve you. You were a better person than me. I miss you, my love." Then, leaning over, he kissed her coffin. It was closed, and yet it was clear he was kissing her forehead.

Turning to his right, he stood before Julia's coffin. The church was heartbreakingly quiet. Daniel placed his right hand on his oldest daughter's coffin and said, "My lovely girl, a life cut short is a brutal thing. A father should never have to bury his daughter, but here I am. Thank you for the immeasurable joy you brought me. I love you now, I loved you then, and I will love you always." Then he leaned over and kissed the coffin.

The church was no longer silent. People were weeping as softly as possible. Daniel was oblivious to the presence of anyone other than his girls.

Standing in front of the third coffin, he placed his right hand on it. He stood there silent for an awkward moment, and then he began to cry. When he spoke, his voice wavered. "My baby girl, how will I ever live without you? Thank you, Jordan. You reminded me of what matters most. I wish I had listened more, but I was a fool. I thought I had more time. I remember how you used to hug me as if you'd never let me go. You'd wrap your arms so tightly around my neck that I could hardly breathe. I'd give anything for one more hug.

"Now I am the one who must let go, and I fear I'm not man enough for the task. I love you. I love you now, I loved you then, and I will love you always." Leaning over, he kissed the coffin, turned, and walked straight down the center aisle and out the doors of the church.

Seconds later, his father followed.

The Pastor finished the service, and the congregation made their way to the cemetery. When they arrived, Daniel was sitting at the graveside in one of the chairs reserved for the family.

The coffins were lowered into the earth, prayers were offered, and Daniel disappeared once again.

Nobody saw or heard from him for three weeks. All attempts to contact him were ignored.

After three weeks, his parents stood at the door of his home as they had done every day since they arrived in town. They knocked long and hard. They knew Daniel wouldn't come to the door. They knew their son. Having knocked enough to get Daniel's attention, his father raised his voice and said, "Son, I know you are in there. I don't know what to say or do. I don't know how to reach you. Suffering has its own timetables and agendas. We will give you the time and space you've requested, but we will be thinking of you every day." Daniel's father paused to catch his breath. He felt old and tired. "Your mother and I are going home today, but we're only two hours away and can come back anytime. Just call."

His fatherly intuition sensed his son on the other side of the door. Lowering his voice slightly, he said, "Please do me one favor, son. Never forget, I love you now, I loved you then, and I will love you always."

It was something he had said to Daniel since he was a little boy, and now he could hear Daniel sobbing on the other side of the door. But still, the door didn't open.

## 5. WHEN NOTHING MAKES SENSE

The weeks passed, but Daniel was nowhere to be seen. The house was still and quiet, every blind and curtain drawn tight. He didn't leave the house, come to the door, or answer his phone. Everyone who knew him was worried about him.

Almost every day, someone would stop by the house, but Daniel didn't come to the door.

"What's he eating? He hasn't been seen coming in or out of that house for two months," someone was overheard saying at the local market. What they didn't know was that around midnight every Monday, Charlie would leave a week's worth of food and other supplies on Daniel's front porch.

Charlie had been his father's best friend since childhood. When he was a child, Daniel used to sit on one of the tired old rocking chairs while his father and Charlie visited. Later, as a teenager, Daniel would stop by and visit Charlie on the way home from school.

One Wednesday afternoon, while most people were at work and the rest of the town was getting on with life, Daniel's front door opened.

Stepping outside, after more than two months in seclusion, he walked the three blocks to Charlie's house, where, as always, Charlie was sitting on his old, weather-beaten cedar rocking chair reading. Charlie was always reading. Looking up, he saw Daniel coming through the front gate and tucked his book between the side of his leg and the arm of the rocking chair.

Daniel was carrying a backpack, but Charlie didn't mention it. In fact, Charlie didn't say anything at all. Not even hello. Nor did Daniel.

Setting his backpack down against the white porch railing, Daniel sat on the other rocking chair next to Charlie, but still no words were exchanged. The two men sat there in silence for a while, rocking back and forth in their chairs. The gentle rock of the chairs was the only sound in the air in the middle of that Wednesday afternoon. After about forty-five minutes, Daniel said, "Thank you." Charlie nodded and replied, "You're welcome."

Another thirty minutes passed in silence. The only noise was the creaking of their rocking chairs. Charlie broke the silence this time. His voice was a deep, warm baritone—reassuring and authoritative. "Setting off on a journey?" he asked.

"Yep."

"Where?"

Daniel didn't reply. He simply pointed toward the mountains above town. He knew Charlie already knew.

"Why?"

"Looking for something."

"What?"

"Answers," Daniel replied. Then he paused for a moment and continued. "Charlie, I know you are the wisest person in town . . ." Charlie raised his hand to interrupt. It was the politest interruption Daniel had ever experienced, and it struck him that in all the years he had been sitting on these rocking chairs, this was the first time Charlie had ever interrupted him.

"If that's true, it's only because your father doesn't live here anymore. He's certainly the wisest man I ever met," said Charlie.

Daniel pressed on "Charlie, I know you've found all your answers on this rocking chair over the years, but I don't think that's gonna work for me. My answers aren't here."

"You won't get any judgment or disagreement from me, kid."

"Kid?"

"Yep. You're still a kid. Your halftime whistle hasn't been blown yet. Life has just dealt you a rough hand—a brutal hand, actually. But kid, you have to admit, up until recently, life was dealing you a whole bunch of aces: magical moments, opportunities, experiences, and incredible people. So, now you have to decide."

"Decide what?" Daniel asked reflexively.

"Continue trying to numb the pain, or enter into it and allow it to transform you. You could drink yourself to death. You could end your life. I know you've considered that. No need to be ashamed. After all you've been through, it's not unusual. Or you could go back to work, lose yourself in that world, and immerse yourself in the debauchery of the big city. Of course, you already know that none of that will satisfy you.

"Suffering gives birth to wisdom or foolishness. You've suffered horrendously, and now you're at a crossroads. But I guess the backpack tells me you've decided something."

"What does it mean to enter into my pain?"

"Well, that's different for everyone. You know there are no cookie-cutter answers here on Charlie's porch. And I know your dad taught you that because he taught me too. You have to find your own answers."

"What answers?"

"Well, I asked what you were looking for and you said 'answers.' But my guess is you haven't met the real Daniel yet, the fullest expression of yourself."

"Huh?"

"Don't get me wrong. You were probably five years old when you first sat on that rocking chair. An hour later, I knew you were an impressive kid. But when we're young, people load us down with expectations born from their own unlived lives. Most of us respond to these expectations by being who other people want us to be. This is natural because we yearn for love, affection, and affirmation.

"So, we learn to please others, and too often we lose ourselves in the bargain. But you aren't a child anymore. It's time to break free from many of those influences and expectations. It's time to work out who you are soul deep."

Charlie and Daniel sat rocking in their chairs for the better part of the afternoon, and then Daniel stood up, hoisted his pack onto his back, and turned to leave. When he got to the bottom of the white steps, without looking back he said, "I'll see you around, Charlie!"

"I sure hope so, kid! But I am old, you are young, and nobody is promised tomorrow."

Daniel almost smiled as he set off on his long walk out of town.

# 6. SAY GOODBYE TO IT ALL

In the afternoon sun, people looked twice at the man walking out of town along Route 12. "Is that Daniel?" they asked each other.

Those who saw him standing at the site of the accident with a backpack at his feet knew for sure. He stood there for almost an hour, observing the crosses, notes, photos, and mountain of flowers. The flowers were dead now, except for three bouquets that had been placed recently.

Daniel looked around, his senses heightened, and images of the past and the present flashed through his mind. There were tire marks on the road, those last pieces of glass that accidents leave behind, and the road was stained with deer blood. He got dizzy for a moment thinking that perhaps the blood stains didn't belong to the deer. Imagining what happened that day, he went into a daze, lost his balance, and stumbled into the road. The booming sound of a horn snapped him out of his daze, and he stepped off the side of the road as a huge truck hurtled past, throwing up dust and spraying him with a gust of greasy wind.

Falling to his knees before the makeshift shrine, Daniel began to weep. He had cried more since that fateful day than he had in his first thirty-three years. When the tears stopped, Daniel stood up, wiped his face dry, hoisted his backpack, and walked out of town, across the bridge, and up into the mountains.

Later that afternoon, a man named Guy Sutherland walked into Murphy's, the bar in the middle of town, and announced, "I saw Daniel walking out of town."

Guy was seventy-two years old, and every day since he'd retired on his sixty-fifth birthday, he'd arrive at the bar at five-thirty, have one beer, then walk home for dinner with his wife.

"Really?" Brian, the bartender, asked. "Are you sure it was him? Where do you think he's going?"

"Well, I didn't talk to him, and I'm still working on my ability to read minds, so I can't be sure, but he looked like he was headed for the mountains."

## 7. THE LETTER

Walking out of town that day, Daniel was more unsure of himself than he had ever been. For the first time in thirty-three years, he didn't have a plan.

It became quickly apparent that his physical condition had deteriorated massively over the past couple of months. Almost ten weeks of drinking himself into a stupor, trying to numb his pain, had left him in a pathetic physical state.

After thirty minutes, Daniel was panting, but he was afraid to stop and rest. If he stopped now, he might turn back. The other thing he became aware of was that he seemed to be rushing. "Why am I in a hurry?" he asked himself.

It was an old habit. Daniel had been in a hurry to get somewhere his whole life. But now he intentionally slowed his pace, saying to himself, "Find a comfortable rhythm, a pace you could sustain indefinitely."

The cool mountain air began to fill his lungs as he got farther from town. "When was the last time I breathed so deeply? When was the last time I was conscious of the breathing that was keeping me alive?"

The doorway to negativity opened in his mind, and the voices of doubt, discouragement, and regret began their incessant chatter. He swatted them away with a litany of small things he was grateful for in that moment. The negativity fled, but he knew it would be back.

A few miles later, he stepped off the road he had been hugging, and made his way onto the hiking path that would lead him deep into the mountains.

People would think he was running away. Daniel knew that. He had written a letter and mailed copies to his parents, Javier, Charlie, other friends and colleagues at work, and Jessica's parents.

The letter read:

*In my teenage years, my father gave me some timeless advice. Whenever you are unsure what to do, he told me, consider if you are running toward something or away from something.*

*The soul-crushing circumstances of these past several weeks have* beckoned me away from this crazy, noisy, busy world. Most people will think I'm running away. It's not that. I hope you know that's not who I am. But I also confess that I don't know what I am running toward.

We go along in life. But if all we do is go along, then that becomes our life. I don't know where I'm going or what I'm doing. All I know is that I cannot just go along anymore.

I may be crazy. Who knows? I might be back in a week having come to that realization. What I know for sure is that I won't be sitting around ten years from now saying, "I wish I had done that."

Thank you for all your love and support, especially over these past few weeks.

*Daniel*

## 8. THE LAST SIGHTING

Daniel walked out of town that afternoon. It was the last time anyone saw him.

## 9. DISAPPEARED

Year after year, the seasons came and went, but nobody saw or heard from Daniel.

## 10. OLD FRIENDS

A few years later, Daniel's father was visiting Charlie on his birthday. They sat on the rocking chairs all afternoon, talking, laughing, remembering.

"I've been going up into the mountains once a week," Daniel's father confessed. "I can't find him, Charlie."

Charlie sensed that Daniel's father wanted to ask him a question, and he knew what the question would be. But Charlie's signature virtue was patience, and he waited.

"Do you think he's still alive?" Daniel's father finally asked.

Charlie replied to his question with the same question. "Do *you* think he's still alive?"

"I do," Daniel's father said.

Charlie nodded quietly for what seemed like a long time, before saying, "Yep, he's alive. You'd know if he wasn't. And I would too."

## 11. THE CAVEMAN

A few weeks later, the whispers began. People reported seeing a vagrant up in the mountains.

Over time, these sightings became more common, especially during the warmer months, and a legend began to develop around this man who lived in the mountains.

The legend grew, and so did the stories, each one more fantastical than the last. And before too long, people started calling the mountain dweller "The Caveman." It stuck.

Folks in town didn't take much notice. Nobody had been hurt, and they were accustomed to hikers coming into town telling stories. But Charlie knew as soon as he heard about "The Caveman." He didn't hear anyone else in town make the connection, or even raise the possibility, but Charlie knew it was Daniel.

It had been years. People had moved on with their lives. Some probably thought Daniel had kept walking, looking for a place where there wasn't a memory around every corner. But Charlie knew, and he knew for sure.

## 12. THE EVENING NEWS

On the evening news a few months later, there was a segment about "The Caveman." Charlie was surprised it had taken this much time.

There wasn't much to report. The Caveman was a mystery, so the news story was full of speculation and raised more questions than it answered. But it was enough to whip people into a frenzy.

One journalist saw an opportunity to make a name for herself and grasped it with both hands. Her name was Melissa Mayer. Tall and blonde, she had that watchable quality that endears news anchors to people.

Every time there was a sighting, she would track down the person who had encountered this so-called caveman and do an interview. She always asked the same two questions: "Did you talk to him?" and "Were you afraid of him?" For months, anyone who had encountered the Caveman answered no to both questions.

The journalist also asked each person to place a pin on a huge map indicating where they had seen him. This concerned Charlie. He knew it was Daniel, and he became uneasy, fearing people might start hunting him. The map in the television studio further stoked the mania, and within a matter of weeks, everyone was talking about this mysterious man in the mountains.

"Why didn't you talk to him?" Melissa Mayer asked one man in his late twenties.

"I'm not sure," he replied.

"Did he look dangerous?"

"No."

"Does he have scars on his face or crazy eyes?" Mayer pressed.

"No."

"Did he do anything that made you feel unsafe?"

Charlie was sitting at home watching the interview. He recognized she was interviewing for pain. She was painting an image of a madman to invoke fear, even though nobody had described the man in these ways.

"Not at all," the young man replied, derailing Mayer. "He was calm and peaceful. He didn't look at us, talk to us, or try to engage us in any way. He was only passing by. But I do wish now that I had spoken to him," he said wistfully.

At that moment, Charlie knew that anyone who saw Daniel in the future would try to talk to him, and that whatever peace he had found in those mountains was coming to an end.

He was right, of course. Charlie usually was. He had a gift. All those afternoons of silence and solitude sitting on his rocking chair had honed his ability to see the essence of things.

A week later, a grainy photo of the Caveman appeared in the media. The quality was horrible, but it confirmed what Charlie already knew. It was Daniel.

Still, nobody else in town seemed to have made the connection. Did they know? Were they merely pretending not to know? Perhaps they were so used to seeing Daniel in those immaculately tailored custom suits that they truly didn't recognize him with the beard hair down to his shoulders. Then again, maybe people didn't want it to be him.

One thing everyone agreed upon was that nobody liked the attention it was bringing to their quiet little town.

## 13. THE HERMIT

The following week there were new reports, and now the pins on Melissa Mayer's map were accompanied by stories of conversations people claimed to have had with the Caveman.

"As I approached him," one man reported, "he stood perfectly still with his eyes cast down toward the ground. A moment later, a handful of lavender butterflies alighted on his right shoulder. He didn't look at them or flinch; it was as if they were a natural part of his day.

I asked him what he was doing up in the mountains, and he looked up at me. I had to take a step back.

"It's not that I was afraid, but his gaze was so powerful, it was as if it pushed me backward. When he answered my question, his voice was calm and melodious, but I have no idea what he said. I could see his lips moving and hear him speaking, but what he actually said, I don't know."

"From afar he looked unkempt," a woman shared, "but up close I realized that, while his beard and hair were long, and his clothes were mismatched, his hygiene was beyond reproach. I thought he would smell horrible, but he didn't. He did smell, but it was the fragrance of wild berries."

"I asked the Caveman some questions," another woman shared. "When I asked how many years he had been in the mountains, he said he didn't know. I asked if he was homeless, and he smiled as if I had told a mildly humorous joke. He has a radiant smile. I mean, at that moment, I had one of the clearest thoughts I've ever had. I thought to myself—he has something I don't have. There was pure joy in his eyes when he smiled, and I wondered when I last smiled like that, with that much uninhibited joy. Hiking back down the mountain, I realized I hadn't experienced that kind of joy since I was about five years old. And I found myself yearning to rediscover that feeling."

A few days later, Melissa Mayer and her crew trekked into the mountains hoping to interview the Caveman. She didn't find him, but she spoke to some people who had seen him that day. One man was visibly shaken. "What happened?" she asked him, pushing the microphone in his face.

"He was sitting on a large rock by the stream when I approached him. I stood about six feet away and started asking him questions. The hermit invited me to sit down next to him and began to tell the story of my life. He knew things that would be impossible for any other human being to know. He knew things about my life, my family, my work, and my past . . . He knew things about me that I have never told anyone!

"I came hiking today because I have a decision to make. It might be the most significant decision of my life. The hermit knew that. I sat there stunned as he described two futures.

"'You have been reflecting on this question for many months,' the hermit said to me. 'It's the biggest decision you will make in your life. Be still, close your eyes, and get lost in the possibilities. Pay attention to the decision you are leaning toward. Don't tell me what it is. Hold it in your mind.'

"After a few minutes of silence, he continued, 'Choose what you are thinking right now, and your future will be the first future I described. Do what you have been thinking of doing for the past three or four weeks, and your future will be the second future I described.'"

"You called him a hermit," Melissa Mayer interjected, as if she hadn't heard his incredible story. "Did he call himself that?" she persisted.

"No. He didn't refer to himself in any way. But I remember thinking he certainly isn't a vagrant. His self-sufficiency alone proves that. When people started calling him the Caveman, I found that derogatory. Whoever this man is, he has an uncommon wisdom that far exceeds education, he has exceptional interpersonal skills, and he has spiritual gifts that defy explanation.

"I called him a hermit out of respect," he said thoughtfully.

Mayer interrupted, "What else do you think people should know about the Caveman?" She was clearly trying to keep that narrative alive.

"All I know is that he's something more than any of us have considered. The way you speak about him is impersonal and dehumanizing. But he isn't an object for our entertainment. He's a person, an incredibly fascinating human being."

Melissa Mayer didn't seem to know what to say, and the interview faded.

## 14. DO YOU THINK IT'S HIM?

The next day, Javier stopped by Charlie's house. Javier and Daniel used to play ball on the street in front of Charlie's house as children with a group of their friends. He knew that Charlie was a man of habits, and this meant that by midafternoon he would find Charlie sitting in his rocking chair on the porch.

Javier also knew that Charlie was a man of few words, so he walked up to the porch, sat in the rocking chair next to Charlie, and waited.

Charlie didn't say anything. This wasn't unusual, but Javier was more impatient than usual today. After fifteen minutes of silence, Javier asked, "Do you think it's him?"

"Yep. I know it is," Charlie replied. "You do too."

"Do you think he's gone crazy up there alone in the mountains?"

"Nope."

"Should I go up there and try and help him?" Javier asked.

Charlie smiled. At first, it was a broad smile, then it turned into a faint chuckle, which quickly became a deep belly laugh. Javier shifted in his chair, unsure whether Charlie would ever stop laughing.

"What's so funny?" Javier inquired, confused.

"Sorry, Javier. I don't hear many jokes here on the porch these days. Is he crazy? No. He's probably the sanest person in the country by now. Does he need your help? No. You've always been a good friend to him, Javier. I remember that, ever since you two were boys, you've been watching out for him. But he doesn't need your help now. In fact, at this point, you may need his help more than he needs yours."

Javier was perplexed. "What do you mean?"

"Javi, have you thought about what it takes to survive up in those mountains all year round? Combine that with the piercing clarity that silence and solitude give birth to, and it's likely our friend has become a highly evolved human being."

The old man sighed. "Do you remember when you and Daniel were kids and you asked me why I spent so much time here on the porch sitting in silence?"

"Sure. It seemed boring to us," Javier replied.

"Do you remember what I told you when you finally worked up the courage to ask the question?" Charlie pressed.

"I've never forgotten," Javier recalled. "'You can learn more in an hour of silence than you can in a year from books.'"

"Exactly. Silence is incredibly powerful. It's one of the main ingredients missing from most unhappy people's lives. But think about it this way, Javi. When you go for a walk on your own, things become clearer in your mind, don't they?"

"Sure," Javier affirmed, still unsure where this was going.

"Now, take the clarity you gain by going for a walk, multiply it by infinity, take it to the heights of eternity, and you'll still have barely a glimpse of the clarity Daniel has acquired up in the mountains."

"Will he come back?"

"Yes," Charlie said confidently and without hesitation.

"How do you know?"

"Two reasons. First, he didn't go into the mountains to hide. He went up there to be healed. And second, there is a purpose to this time in Daniel's life beyond his own needs. Whatever gifts he has received up there, people need down here, and he will be led back to share them when the time is right."

The two men sat quietly for a while, and then Charlie continued. "The thing is, every tribe, culture, and society, needs people to do exactly what Daniel has done. We can't all go off into the mountains for years at a time to work things out, but we need someone among us to do it. The problem is, we want our spiritual leaders to be like us, so we never give them the time or space to receive the clarity necessary to lead.

"Every society needs people to do the kind of inner work Daniel has been doing. Everyone benefits from it. That's how cultures ascend. Our society doesn't value inner work. That's why we are devolving as a society and descending into cultural oblivion.

"So, yes, he will come back. He will come back to share what he has learned. He will come back to share who he has become. He may be very different from how you remember, but he will come back. You can be sure of that."

"When?" Javier asked.

"Well, a month ago, I would've said when he was good and ready. But with all that's been going on, I suspect they will drive him out of those mountains sooner rather than later."

"Charlie, can I ask you one more thing?"

"Sure, anything."

"Why haven't the people here in town worked out that it's him?"

"Ah, that's a complicated question, my young friend," Charlie said. "What I mean is, there is more than one answer. Some don't want to work it out. Some don't want anyone else to work it out. Some are afraid to admit what they already know to be true. They don't want their quiet little town to become a circus. But regardless of any of that, the fact that people are not talking about him isn't healthy, and it's a sure sign that a storm is brewing."

They sat quietly for some time before Javier asked, "Are you worried about him?"

"Sure," Charlie replied with a simplicity that highlighted his authenticity. "Think about it. Dozens of people have encountered him now. They've asked him all sorts of questions. But nobody has asked him his name. That's the essential problem with fame: It's dehumanizing. They don't see Daniel as a person, and that never ends well."

Driving home, Javier mulled over the conversation. He yearned for more of the wisdom Charlie had accumulated over the years and resolved to spend a few minutes each day in the classroom of silence.

## 15. HEALING AND HYSTERIA

The hysteria broke out a month later.

A woman drove her sick daughter more than a thousand miles, carried her seven-year-old girl on her back up into the mountains, and searched for the hermit.

When she found him in the mountains, she begged him to heal her daughter.

"I've never done anything like that before," he explained. But the mother threw herself at his feet and kept pleading with him.

"What makes you think I'm even capable of such a thing?" the hermit asked.

"I know you are. I can't explain it, but in my heart, I know it's true—even if you don't know it yourself," the desperate mother replied.

The hermit heard the voice saying, "Sometimes other people know things about us long before we know them about ourselves. Their belief in us reveals our unexplored potential."

"How can I serve you?" Daniel asked quietly.

The mother got up, carried her little girl about twenty feet away, and set her down gently on a patch of grass. "Rest here for a minute, Mia." The child was clearly exhausted, limp from head to toe, and didn't look like she could muster the energy to even sit up.

The hermit realized the mother was setting the girl far enough away so she wouldn't overhear their conversation. When the woman returned, she whispered to him as she began to weep softly, "My daughter has a very rare blood disease. The doctors say there is nothing more they can do and that she has less than six weeks to live."

"I heard you call your daughter Mia. What's your name?" the hermit asked the mother.

"Ava," she replied.

"Why do you think I can help you?" he inquired.

"It's a sense I have. I may be wrong, but if you had a daughter, wouldn't you try everything you could to help her live?"

Ava's question knocked the wind out of him, and the color drained from his face. It felt like a huge man had punched him deep in his stomach.

For years now, the voice within Daniel had been growing stronger and crisper, and now it said to him, "Do not be afraid!"

"Besides," Ava continued, oblivious to his inner communion, "you are obviously a prophet, a wise man, a visionary, a holy man, one of the enlightened ones. You have been touched by God. All I'm asking is that you place your hands on my daughter and offer a prayer. God favors you, and I am begging you to ask Him to heal her."

The hermit felt uneasy for the first time in longer than he could remember. He disagreed with so much of what the woman was saying, but he had no desire to argue. He had recently resigned himself to being misunderstood.

He took a moment to think and then replied, "Ava, I'm none of those things you described. People are sensationalizing the stories about their experiences up here. I'm not a prophet or a wise man or a visionary or a holy man or any of the things people call me. I'm just a wounded soul."

"What are you afraid of?" Ava asked, raising her voice.

"I'm afraid you will place your hope in me and that you will be disappointed," the hermit explained frankly.

"I don't think that's it," the woman ventured boldly. "I think you are afraid that you have the gift of healing. I think, like us all, you are afraid of your light. There is greatness within you. You know it, and I know it. Besides, Mia has everything to gain and nothing to lose."

There was a growing tension. The moment lingered. But the mother knew instinctively not to interrupt the unfolding moment.

He heard the voice again: "Do not be afraid!"

"Very well," the hermit said softly, surrendering to the situation. "I'll do as you ask, because I feel your anguish deep in my soul, but I have some conditions."

"What kind of conditions?" Ava asked, surprised.

"You say I have been touched by God. This is true, but no more than you or anybody else. How can we not be? It is in God that we live and move and have our being. So, we will pray over your daughter together. This way, if something miraculous does happen, it will have been done through both of us."

"What are your other conditions?"

The hermit knew the girl would be cured. His intuition had become razor-sharp during his time in the mountains. He also knew what the girl's healing would mean.

"Whatever happens, I would like to ask you not to mention this to anyone," he said, looking deep into Ava's eyes. But even as she agreed, he knew she would be on the evening news tomorrow. He bore no ill will toward her. He had lived an unconscious life himself for many years, and he knew that most of what people say and do is said and done unconsciously.

Walking over toward the grass where the little girl was lying, the hermit said to her, "Do you like chocolate, Mia?" A whisper of a smile ran along her lips, and she nodded almost imperceptibly.

The hermit removed a chocolate bar from a pocket somewhere inside his tattered clothing. Ava noticed it was immaculate. It looked like it was straight off the shelf in a store. He went to hand it to Mia, but her mother intercepted it. She unwrapped one end, broke off a piece, and passed it to her daughter.

Ava noticed that the chocolate bar was cold, as if it had been refrigerated. She knew it was over eighty-five degrees that day, and she knew that the hermit's body temperature alone should have melted it in his pocket.

The little girl delighted in the taste.

"Where did you get the chocolate?" Ava asked. But he didn't answer. He was completely focused on the little girl now.

"Mia, do you think you could stand up?"

She shook her head and mumbled, "Too tired."

"Your mom and I will help you. You can lean against that tree over there," he said, trying to encourage her.

The child was seven years old, but she was as fragile as a ninety-year-old woman. Her mother lifted her and carried her over to the tree. It took all of Mia's strength to stay upright, even leaning against the tree.

The hermit laid one hand on the little girl's head and the other on her right shoulder and asked her mother to do the same. Now he began to mumble some words. He spoke so softly that even Mia and her mother could not hear what he was saying. A moment later, Ava broke down, like dam walls cracking, and she began to cry out hysterically, begging God, pleading for her daughter to be cured.

This went on for three minutes. The hermit continued to mumble quietly. Then, crouching down, he held the girl's hands, looked deep into her eyes, and said, "Mia, you are a wonderful young lady, and I have enjoyed meeting you. I can see you have great courage, but I can also see that you are afraid. Don't be afraid. Your mother loves you very much. She carried you all the way up here into the mountains. Why don't you try to take a few steps down the path?"

Mia smiled and began to limp down the hiking path, tentatively at first, but within minutes she had her confidence back and found her stride. Her mother stared at her in amazement. Unable to take her eyes off her daughter, she couldn't believe what she was seeing. Turning around to thank the hermit, she discovered he had disappeared.

"Thank you—" she called out. But there was no reply.

The hermit had healed the girl. At least, that's what people would believe. And everything was about to change.

## 16. THE WORLD BEATS A PATH

The whole world would beat a path to the hermit's cave now. He knew that. There was nothing he could do to stop it.

So, Daniel started wondering where he should go and what he should do. He knew he couldn't stay where he was. Should he go deeper into the mountains and make it harder for people to find him? That felt like running away. Perhaps he had spent enough time in the mountains.

At that moment, a vision of Charlie's rocking chair flashed through Daniel's mind. He wondered what this vision was trying to tell him.

## 17. AN INSTINCT TO RETURN

Daniel woke earlier than usual the next morning. It wasn't yet dawn. It was still dark, and the darkness clung to the morning like a frightened child clings to his mother's leg.

When he opened his eyes, a young boy was standing over him. As he wiped the sleep from his eyes, he realized it was an apparition of his seven-year-old self.

"It's time," the boy said.

"Time for what?" Daniel asked, even though he knew. But the boy said nothing in reply as he faded from sight.

It was time. Daniel knew it. He recalled the fear he'd felt the day he started walking into the mountains years ago. He wasn't afraid anymore. He was at peace. He had learned to inhabit himself. He knew who he was and who he wasn't, and he had embraced the wisdom of acceptance.

Less than an hour later, he started walking out of the mountains. No backpack. Nothing but the mismatched clothes on his back.

Just before eleven o'clock that morning, Daniel arrived in town. His first stop would be Charlie's house. But when he arrived, Charlie wasn't in his rocking chair. Unusual for a Saturday morning.

Daniel walked up the six steps to the porch, remembering how those steps had seemed like the biggest steps in the world when he was a child. When he reached the top, he walked toward the front door and knocked. Charlie didn't like doorbells.

Nobody answered. The town seemed eerily quiet, Daniel realized. There were no cars driving down the street and no children playing catch.

He went next door and knocked, but again nobody answered. As Daniel walked down the street, no one seemed to be around. There was nobody gardening, nobody reading newspapers on front porches, and nobody walking their dogs. When he got to the end of the street, he discovered why.

The cross street led into town, and on the northern side of the town square was the Church of Saint Paul. There were cars parked everywhere, and even from three blocks away, Daniel could see that the church was overflowing with people.

Charlie was dead.

As sure as he knew his right from his left, Daniel knew he was walking toward Charlie's funeral. As he arrived at the church, he tried to gently make his way through the crowd. The first couple he moved past resisted, making comments about him cutting ahead of them. The next group of people looked at him disparagingly. But very quickly people realized it was the hermit, and the crowd parted like the Red Sea for Moses.

At the top of the stairs, one of the ushers blocked his way, thinking he was a homeless person. Daniel stepped to go around him, but the usher stepped to his right, again blocking his way. "This is no place for you today. On any other day, I'd gladly let you come in out of the heat, but not today."

The funeral had not yet begun, and Daniel said quietly, "Please step aside, sir. I'm a friend of the deceased." He spoke softly, but his voice was firm and full of authority, and people turned to see what was happening.

Until then, Daniel had kept his gaze down, but at that moment he lifted his face and looked toward the front of the church, where his eyes locked with his father's. At that moment his father made his way down the aisle as quickly as he could without disrespecting the occasion.

"It's okay, Sean. That's my boy, Daniel."

Sean fumbled an embarrassed apology. "I'm very sorry, Daniel, I didn't recognize you."

Daniel and his father embraced, both men holding on a little longer and a little tighter than usual. Then, turning around, they walked down the aisle to the front row.

The church lit up with whispers. But a few minutes later, the Pastor began the service and a reverent hush fell over the church.

Daniel looked at the casket and began having flashbacks of the last time he had been here in this church. His hands got clammy, his forehead began to sweat, and within minutes he was grief-stricken and spiraling into claustrophobia.

He closed his eyes, thinking it might help, but now all he could see were his wife and daughters' three white coffins. He opened his eyes with a start, and his mother took his hand in hers and said gently, "Breathe. Breathe."

Her boy was back. Tears began to stream down her face.

The Pastor started speaking about Charlie, and that mercifully refocused Daniel on the proceedings at hand. He thought about the first time he had struggled to climb up onto the rocking chair next to Charlie's, and all the afternoons he had spent sitting there talking to him.

Daniel felt the familiar ache of grief, but there was no tragedy in Charlie's death. He had lived a rich, full life. But the girls . . . their lives had been cut short. Such a sharp turn in life. The devastation of unexpected death is different.

On the day he buried his wife and daughters, death felt like a thief. Today, death was a friend, ushering Charlie from this life to the next. Few men have lived so intentionally, so engaged with all of life. Charlie's was a life well spent.

# 18. HOMECOMING

While the pallbearers carried Charlie's casket down the aisle, Daniel slipped out the side door of the church. He walked to Charlie's house and sat on the rocking chair. After a while, his father joined him.

"Thought I might find you here," his father said.

"Yeah, I wasn't sure what beckoned me down from the mountains this morning, but I'm glad I was here. Wish I had come earlier. Wish I could have one last conversation with Charlie. Wish I could just sit next to him and rock in silence," Daniel shared.

"He was a fine man, son. He lived a thoughtful life. And while that might seem like a small thing, it's harder than you'd think. Too often people sleepwalk through life. A thoughtful life is rare and beautiful," his father concluded reverently.

Daniel nodded his head. He had experienced both sides of consciousness now, and he knew what his father was saying. But before he went into the mountains, his father's words wouldn't have registered.

"As a kid, I spent a lot of time wondering what Charlie was thinking when he sat here on this porch," Daniel said. "I'd ask him over and again, 'What are you thinking, Charlie?' For years he would just smile. Then, I remember once, when I was about nine years old, I asked him again. He said to me, 'You are old enough to start taking your own thoughts seriously, Daniel. It's time to stop wondering what I'm thinking. You have your own thinking to do.'"

Daniel and his father sat sharing their favorite memories of Charlie, and then they rocked quietly in their chairs for almost an hour.

"You must be getting tired," Daniel's father finally said to his son.

Daniel smiled.

"Anyway, my boy, there is so much I'd like to talk about, but you should get some rest." And with that, he passed his son a set of keys.

"What are these?" Daniel asked.

"The keys to your new home. Charlie left this place to you."

"Really?"

"Indeed, he did."

"How did he know I'd come back?" Daniel asked.

Tears formed in his father's eyes, but they lingered on the edges of his eyelids. "Not sure. But he was confident that you would. In fact, it was only three weeks ago he told me, 'It won't be long now.'"

Daniel smiled again. "He had an uncanny intuition, didn't he?" His father nodded his head gently in thoughtful affirmation.

"Thanks, Dad. I know it probably feels like I abandoned you and Mom—"

His father raised his hand to interrupt Daniel, just like Charlie had the day he left for the mountains, and said, "Your mother and I don't feel that way. We've always encouraged you to find your own path and follow it. That wasn't going to change now. We missed you, of course. We were concerned about you. But what we wanted, more than anything for ourselves, was whatever would ease your pain and bring you healing."

Daniel nodded appreciatively and smiled. *To love is to will the good of the other*, he thought. It was something his father had said to him dozens of times throughout his life.

"I haven't seen you smile like that since you were a child," his father said. "I'm so happy to see you, son."

The two men stood, and Daniel hugged his father tight. "Thank you, Dad."

"For what?"

"Everything, Dad. Everything."

## 19. EZRA'S DREAM

An hour after his father left, Daniel heard a knock on the door. It startled him. It was such an ordinary thing, but he had become delightfully unaccustomed to such things in the mountains. He wondered how long it would take for him to get used to the ordinary things of everyday life again. He hoped he would never get used to some of them.

On the other side of the door was Ezra Abrams. Since Daniel was a child, Ezra had been his family's attorney.

"Hello, Mr. Abrams," Daniel said, pleased to see him.

"Hello, Daniel. I can see your dad has told you about Charlie's gift of the house, but there are a few other things I'd like to go through with you. If you have a few minutes."

"Sure," Daniel replied.

"Can I come in?" Ezra asked.

"Yes, yes, of course, please," Daniel said as he fumbled another ordinary situation.

Ezra and Daniel sat down in the living room. Opening his briefcase, the attorney began to speak. "After you went away, Daniel, your family appointed me as the custodian of your legal and financial affairs. After some time, your home was considered abandoned and sold. The proceeds were invested with your other assets. Your father, Javier, and I packed everything up and put it in storage.

"If you can be content living a simple life, you have enough money to live that way for many years. I have never charged any fees. It didn't seem right. Your father insisted, but for once in my life, I ignored him."

"You didn't need to do that, Ezra. Please take whatever is due to you with interest," Daniel replied.

"I wouldn't dream of it!" Ezra insisted.

"That's an interesting word choice," Daniel commented.

"What do you mean?"

"Dream. You said you wouldn't dream of it," Daniel explained.

"Sure, it's only an expression."

"I know, but as you said it, an idea crossed my mind," Daniel explained.

"What's that?"

"My father told me once that you didn't want to be a lawyer. He told me your dream was to have a coffee shop with baked goods and books, a place where people could meet and connect."

"Every man should have a dream, don't you think?" Ezra mused.

"I do, my old friend, but there's more to it. When a man has a chance to follow his dream, he should grasp that opportunity with both hands."

"You're probably right Daniel, but that opportunity never really presented itself, and I'm busy with so many other things," Ezra replied.

"I understand," Daniel said before pressing on. "Many people stay busy enough to avoid their dreams for a whole lifetime."

"I wouldn't know where to start," Ezra exclaimed.

"It is written: 'If you want to build a ship, don't drum up the men to gather wood, divide the work, and give orders. Instead, teach them to yearn for the vast and endless sea.'"

"I'm not a young man anymore," Ezra replied.

"Exactly, so you have no time to waste," Daniel insisted and continued, "There are two times in life when we can pursue our dreams with reckless abandon. The first is when we are young, before we become entangled in the responsibilities of marriage and family. The second is when we are older and have largely fulfilled these responsibilities."

Daniel had been gone for years, but Ezra had also known him since he was a boy. And even with all that hair on his face, Ezra could see the twinkle in Daniel's eyes, and he knew he was hatching a plan.

"I noticed that the old bakery building on the south side of the square is available," Daniel said, continuing his train of thought. "It's the perfect size for your dream."

"I don't understand," Ezra said, confused.

"Well, let's just say that I have decided to stay here in town, to live here in Charlie's old house, and make myself available to anyone who comes to visit. So, we can finish any other business you have for me some other day because right now, I want you to drive over to the realtor's office and lease that building. People will start coming to visit soon and they will need a place to gather—a place like the one you've always dreamed of opening," Daniel said, smiling broadly.

Ezra was hesitant. Daniel sensed his resistance. But he also knew if the moment passed, this opportunity would be gone forever, and so would Ezra's dream. He could see the struggle taking place within the older man's heart. And so, he sat quietly, watching, waiting, letting it play out in Ezra's heart.

Then, at the right moment, in a softer, gentler voice, Daniel spoke again.

"It is written: 'Your dreams are your dreams for a reason. Beware resistance. Beware the desire to delay something you know you should be doing right now.'"

"Okay, okay," Ezra said, finally surrendering. He had been wrestling with this dream his whole life. The struggle had been with himself, with all the expectations people had burdened him with, with his desire to please others, and with the fear and doubt that any man needs to overcome to boldly follow his dream. His destiny had finally gotten the upper hand.

When he woke that morning, Ezra never could have imagined that his life would change so magnificently in a single day.

## 20. CRAZY OLD MAN

"What have you gone and done?" Leah asked loudly from the kitchen as Ezra walked through the front door that evening. They had been married for over forty years, and she already knew that he had leased the building without a whisper of the idea to her. It was a small town.

"What do you mean?" Ezra asked sheepishly.

"You know exactly what I mean, Mr. Ezra Abrams."

"Well, it's a good thing half the residents of this town are not lawyers; otherwise, they would be in jail for failing to keep attorney-client privilege. Can anyone in this town keep anything to themselves?" Ezra deflected.

"You're avoiding my question," Leah said. This was one of the many things Ezra loved about his wife. She could tease him and hold him accountable all at once. Of course, sometimes he hated it too.

"An opportunity came up. I have served my clients faithfully, fulfilled the hopes my father had for his son, provided for my family, and now it's time to pursue my dream," Ezra explained.

"You silly old man," Leah said with love and humor. "Fewer people come here every year! Who is going to buy your coffee and cakes?"

"Even if very few people come to the shop, what does it matter, my dear? We live simply, we have all we need, and it will make an old man very happy," said Ezra.

"When will you open this coffee shop?" Leah inquired.

"Hmmm . . . I was thinking maybe . . . Saturday?"

"You *have* gone crazy, Ezra. What's really going on?"

"It's never good to unnecessarily delay a dream, and I think we both know I've been doing that for far too many years. I was thinking we would go into the city tomorrow for a coffee maker, a refrigerator, some tables and chairs, and a makeshift countertop to get us started."

Leah put her hands on her hips and said, "We? Us?"

"Yes, we!" he said with the boyish smile she had always loved, gesturing with his hands, back and forth, between himself and Leah. "All these years we have been doing our own things, and I was hoping that now we could do something together!"

She walked over to him, took his face in her gorgeous old hands, and said, "You are a good man, Ezra Abrams, and you deserve this." Then she put her arms around his neck and hugged the only man she had ever loved.

"What about supplies?" she asked.

"Coffee we can bring back from the city with a bunch of cold drinks. On Friday, I was hoping you could help me bake some cakes and cookies in time for a Saturday opening. And finally, I thought I would bring that old bookcase from the garage and all those books from the basement. We can start with those until I can organize a book supplier," Ezra explained.

"How will people know *we* are open for business?" Leah quizzed him.

Ezra noted the "we" and his happiness expanded. "I stopped by Owen's sign shop today and ordered a temporary sign," he replied.

"Well, you have just thought of everything," Leah teased again. "What does this temporary sign say?"

"EZRA'S—Coffee and Cakes!"

"What about your law practice? Your clients?" Leah asked.

"Details, woman, details," Ezra said, knowing that she hated being called that, as if she were a great figure from the Old Testament.

Leah shook her head and smiled at him as she went back to doing what she had been doing before Ezra arrived home.

# 21. ASKING FOR HELP

The following morning, Daniel got his beard under control, had his first hot shower in years, put on some clean clothes, and walked over to Sean Murphy's house.

People called him Murph. He was your quintessential Irish character. At just over six feet tall and almost three hundred pounds, with his curly ginger hair and beard, he was an imposing figure. He had never set foot in the homeland of his ancestors, but he had a thick Irish brogue and a fabulous sense of humor. Both had been passed to him by his parents and grandparents.

Daniel knocked, and Sean answered the door a few moments later.

A look of embarrassment came across his face as soon as he saw Daniel, and Sean's big, fair Irish cheeks turned red. "I'm so sorry, Daniel," he said, with his eyes firmly planted in the direction of his shoes. "If I'd known it was you . . ."

"No apology necessary. It's important to keep the riffraff out of a solemn occasion like Charlie's funeral," Daniel said, smiling. Sean smiled back, and they both began to laugh.

Sean had a boisterous and contagious laugh, but it struck Daniel that he had no memory of ever hearing him laugh before that moment.

Both Sean and Ezra had sons a couple of years ahead of Daniel in school. Both boys had overdosed and died, about three months apart, when they were twenty-one years old. Ezra had thrown himself into his work. Sean had thrown himself into the bottle and fallen into a deep depression. Daniel was reminded that he wasn't the only person in this town who had been struck by tragedy. It was easy to see the town as idyllic, but life is messy wherever you go.

"So, how can I help you?" Sean asked.

"I've decided to stay here in town, Sean, which means we'll likely see a steady stream of visitors around here. During my last weeks in the mountains, people came to visit every day. Now that they don't have to make the hike to see me, I suspect the number of visitors will only increase."

"I'm sure you're right, Daniel," Sean confirmed.

"You did a pretty good job of keeping me out of church the other day, and you did it in a calm and dignified way. So I was wondering if you'd be willing to come over to the house and keep things orderly. I was thinking that perhaps we could enlist a couple of the other retired guys in town to help."

"I'd be happy to, Danny," Sean replied. He was the only person other than Daniel's mother who called him that. "When do you think people will start showing up?"

"I'd say by Saturday people will have worked out I'm here. I'm planning to sit on Charlie's famous rocking chair and visit with people one at a time."

Daniel saw that the Irishman seemed distracted. "What is it, Sean?"

"Why did you decide to come back now?" he asked Daniel.

"There were a few reasons. People had discovered where I was living in the mountains, and more people were coming every day. I didn't go up there to run away, and I didn't want to start hiding. I also never intended to stay up there forever, so it seemed like the right time to come home."

Daniel knew Sean had another question, so he asked, "What else?"

"No, nothing," Sean mumbled.

"I can tell you want to ask something else," Daniel pressed him gently.

"Alright. Did you . . . did you really heal that little girl?"

"I don't know what happened," Daniel began. "There are few things more powerful in the universe than a mother's love, and the love that mother had for her child was breathtaking. Her journey into the mountains was an incredible act of faith. And the thing is, she believed something extraordinary was going to happen.

"At first, I said no, but she persisted. I continued to resist, but then I had this blinding awareness that I was resisting for all the wrong reasons. I was focused on myself. So, I surrendered to the moment, turned my focus to the little girl, and reminded myself that we can all be instruments of goodness, kindness, and healing."

"How did you do it? I mean, what happened?" Sean asked.

"I placed one hand on the little girl's head and the other on her shoulder, and I prayed. I prayed that the mother's strength, courage, and goodness would flow into her little girl. I prayed that my own health and goodness would flow into her. I prayed that my daughters' goodness would flow into her and give her new life. I called on the best of humanity from every age and begged them to allow their goodness to flow into the girl. And finally, I begged God to immerse her in His goodness and unleash His healing powers."

"That's the mumbling the mother described on the news?" Sean asked.

Daniel nodded, recalling the power of that moment, before asking, "What do you think happened?"

Sean thought for a moment, then said, "The doctors confirmed it was miraculous. I think you have somehow developed a rare connection with God, and I think God healed that little girl through you," Sean explained.

"It's a beautiful mystery," Daniel said, nodding slowly. "Our lust to understand all things and our rejection of things we cannot see or explain are among the curses of our age. We are surrounded by mystery and miracles. If we're unwilling to acknowledge the mystery around us, we become incapable of cherishing the miracles within us.

"It is written: 'There are only two ways to live your life. One is as though nothing is a miracle. The other is as though everything is a miracle.'"

*Daniel had changed*, Sean thought to himself. Like many others in town, he had known Daniel before he went into the mountains, but the man standing before him now possessed uncommon wisdom.

"Thank you for asking me, Daniel, it's an honor. I'll see you Saturday."

Daniel started to leave, but when he got to the middle of the road, he stopped and turned back toward Sean. "There is one other thing it could've been, Murph," he called out.

"What's that?" Sean called back.

"It could've been the chocolate," Daniel said jovially, and both men smiled.

Daniel walked home, and Sean was glad he hadn't lost his sense of humor up in the mountains.

## 22. MIDLIFE CRISIS

People found Daniel even faster than he thought they would. Turning onto his street on his way back from Sean's house, he noticed half a dozen people were standing on the sidewalk outside his new home. He asked his first visitors to make themselves comfortable on the front lawn and invited the first person in line onto the porch to visit with him.

"What's your name?" Daniel asked his first visitor as the young man sat down in the rocking chair next to him.

"Jacob."

"Where are you from?"

"Outside Pittsburgh."

"What brings you here today, Jacob?" Daniel asked.

"I think I'm having a midlife crisis."

"What makes you think that?"

"Life doesn't make sense anymore. The things I once enjoyed doing aren't interesting anymore. I'm confused. I don't know what I want. I'm having trouble sleeping. I've been drinking too much. I don't like my job anymore. And my wife and I are struggling to connect," Jacob explained in one breath.

"Why do you think society calls it a midlife crisis?" Daniel asked.

Jacob wasn't expecting to be asked questions, and it took him a moment to recalibrate. "Maybe because everything seems to be . . . falling apart?"

"I think you're right," Daniel affirmed. "Everything may *seem* to be falling apart, but what was holding it all together?"

Daniel let the question hang in the air for a couple of minutes before continuing. "Looking back on my own life, before I went into the mountains, I now realize that my ego was working overtime, trying desperately to hold everything together. I think what happens during the middle passage of life is that our ego, finally exhausted, lets go. That's when we start to feel that everything is falling apart."

Jacob was looking at him intently, and Daniel continued, "When I was working on Wall Street, there was this saying: 'A recession is a terrible thing to waste.' I think a similar truth applies here: A midlife crisis is a horrible thing to waste. If we look at it in that context, we begin to wonder if it's a crisis at all. Maybe it's an opportunity . . ."

"What do you mean?" Jacob interjected.

"Let's think about those two words for a moment. A *crisis* is a time of intense turmoil and difficulty. An *opportunity* is a set of circumstances that emerge to make something new possible.

"Words are powerful. These two words—*crisis* and *opportunity*—hold very different energy. If you sat in that rocking chair for the next hour, closed your eyes, and repeated the word *crisis* over and over again in your mind, how do you think you would feel at the end of the hour?"

"Exhausted, anxious . . . depressed," Jacob answered.

"Are these the feelings that pressed you to get in your car and drive five hours to visit me?"

"Yes, yes, exactly," Jacob stammered.

"Now, let me ask you another question. If you sat in that rocking chair for the next hour, closed your eyes, and repeated the word *opportunity* over and over again in your mind, how do you think you would feel at the end of the hour?"

"Better than I have in years," Jacob answered reflectively.

"Our lives are full of opportunities we don't see. As we make our way through the midlife passage, we begin to question all the expectations we have allowed to shape our lives. Some of those burdensome expectations we received from our parents, teachers, friends, and society. Others we placed upon ourselves. So, is this a crisis or an opportunity?" Daniel asked rhetorically. "You get to decide. You can have a midlife crisis or a midlife opportunity. You get to choose."

"So, what do I do?" Jacob asked.

"That's up to you. You can double down and keep doing what you're doing. Plenty of people try that path, but that's exhausting. Pretending always is. Or you can begin paying attention to what's happening within you."

"Is there a question I should be asking myself?"

Daniel thought on this for quite a while. "Some questions to consider: Who are you beyond the labels the world places on you? In what ways are you being summoned to grow? You are a son, a brother, a husband, a father, an employee, et cetera. But before any of that, you are a person, an individual on a unique quest. Who is that unique human being?

"This inner conflict you are experiencing has purpose. It's helping you to discover your unrealized potential. To grow, you will need to set aside the expectations that have directed your life up until this point, acknowledge the ways you sabotage yourself, and set aside your desire for approval. At almost every turn, you will question whether you have the soul strength to walk the path you are being invited to explore."

"What's the biggest mistake I could make?" Jacob asked now.

"During times of inner turbulence, we are drawn to the distraction of external activity. The midlife experience is an interior experience. Resist the temptation to look for external solutions to this internal dilemma."

"What about my marriage?"

"In the middle passage of life, it's easy to fall into taking people and things for granted. Go home, tell your wife you love her, apologize for whatever it is you need to apologize for, share some of your favorite memories of your life together, and then take her to bed—and make love to her as if it were the first time, the last time, and the only time."

Jacob looked at Daniel in astonishment. "Thank you," he said in a bit of a daze. Then he nodded resolutely, stood, and extended his hand to shake with Daniel.

"You're very welcome," Daniel replied, and out of the corner of his eye, he saw the next person eagerly making her way toward the rocking chair.

By the middle of the afternoon, Daniel had finished visiting with everyone who had been waiting on the lawn. He went inside and sat down to read. Hours later he woke, with a disheveled book tickling his neck.

# 23. THE EXTRAORDINARY ORDINARY

Before too long, people were arriving a dozen at a time. "Where does the prophet live?" they asked the locals. Daniel didn't like the name, but he had made peace with the realization that this was one of many things that were beyond his control.

Every week more people came than the week before. Late one afternoon, Ezra stopped by to see how Daniel was doing with the growing crowds. They talked for a while, and then Ezra said, "We've become good friends these past few months, Daniel, and it's a friendship I cherish. But there is a question I can't seem to set out of my mind."

"Go ahead, Ezra. You can ask me anything," Daniel said, warmly inviting him to speak.

Ezra sighed, and Daniel didn't know what to expect. "I've heard you say that you are an ordinary man. Do you really believe that?"

"I do."

"But how can you possibly believe that, Daniel?" Ezra said, exasperated.

Now it was Daniel's turn to sigh.

"Throughout history, most problems have been caused by a single idea: the idea that some people are different. But the minute we start thinking we are different, or others are different, divisions emerge, and that's when things begin to deteriorate.

"All human interaction is rooted in either acceptance or judgment. Acceptance leads human beings to flourish; judgment causes us to wither. When we believe that we are more intelligent, of higher character, better parents, more important, better-looking, more religious, or superior citizens, we place comparison and judgment at the center of the way we relate to others."

"What is the key to this acceptance you speak of?" Ezra asked now.

"It is written: 'We are one.'

"The key to accepting people is to realize that how you treat me is how you treat yourself. What I do to you, I do to myself," Daniel explained.

"How do we tame our judgment?" Ezra asked.

"Suppose we were to assess two people without any judgment or bias. Is that even possible? Only if we begin with the belief that both people are infinitely valuable. This belief allows us to seek and find what is marvelously unique in each person." Daniel noticed that Ezra looked confused, so he paused.

"I'm not sure I understand," Ezra confessed. "We were talking about you and your gifts."

"It's about potential. You cannot separate a person from his or her future potential. When we do, we are ignoring a huge part of that person, possibly the most important aspects. Judging other people is a potential excluding error. Parents marvel at their children's potential, but as adults, we stop considering our own potential and the potential of others who cross our paths.

"Potential is an amazing thing. You are not what has happened to you. You are not what you have accomplished. You are so much more. Even who you are today is only a portion of who you can become. It is impossible to know a person in any meaningful way without considering that person's unrealized potential. When we judge people, we exclude their potential. We use our preferences, biases, and prejudices to define them as more or less, better or worse, or different than us."

The look on Ezra's face told Daniel that he was enjoying the conversation but wasn't sure how all this related to his question.

"When our children died, we didn't only mourn our past with them—we mourned the stolen future. Even today, after all these years, we continue to mourn what could have been. Accidents killed them, and in that moment, fate murdered their potential."

Ezra had a look of dissatisfaction on his face, so Daniel made one last effort to help him understand.

"Think about your own life since I returned to town. It's been an amazing journey. I have heard you tell the story to people, and when you tell it, you are still in awe. You ask about me, but the answer lies within you. How many men at your age would've done what you've done this past year? At any age, actually? Does that mean you are better than other people? No. You have simply realized your potential more at this moment in time."

"But it wouldn't have happened without you!" the older man exclaimed.

"You may be right, but why does that matter? A flower doesn't deny its beauty because it needs sunlight and water," Daniel said with his signature calm assurance.

"So, to answer your question: Do I believe I'm an ordinary man? I do. Has more of my potential been activated at this particular moment in time than others? Yes, I think that's true, but I'm not doing anything others aren't capable of themselves. Many people would look at your transformation over the past year and say it's extraordinary. I believe that is true, but others are capable of the same. I guess, the point is, I'm happy to be ordinary or extraordinary, as long as everyone else is too!"

Ezra smiled, and Daniel reached out and cupped the side of his face with his large right hand.

"It's the generosity and kindness of the so-called ordinary people that make the world go round. I like to think of them as the extraordinary ordinary," Daniel said. "We are part of the extraordinary ordinary, Ezra. There are no ordinary people. Every person is an infinite miracle bubbling with unimagined possibilities."

Ezra nodded his head in agreement and surrender. He knew Daniel had changed, and he felt honored to have him as a friend. It was clearer than ever that the experience in the mountains had transformed him profoundly, and that the world desperately needed the message he had brought back with him.

"I'm sorry, Daniel, I can't seem to let this one go. One more question: How do we live this wisdom in our daily lives?"

"You are a beautiful soul, Ezra," Daniel said, smiling. "Love the unrealized potential in other people. Honor your own potential by remembering that who you are today is but a dim reflection of all you can become. Potential that is honored, loved, and encouraged will flourish."

## 24. AWARENESS

By the time the last visitor left the porch on Saturday night, it was late. Inside, Daniel made himself a sandwich and sat at his kitchen table savoring every bite. It tasted amazing. "It's a simple sandwich," he told himself. But food had never tasted so good.

All his senses had been heightened, transforming even the simplest things into elevated experiences. He was hyperaware of everything happening around and within him. Every breath of fresh air, every tall glass of water, every hot shower, every smile, and every touch. Everything was different.

Daniel wanted others to experience life the way he was experiencing it now. This was his reason. This was why he returned from the mountains. He wanted to share the euphoria he had found in the ordinary things of everyday life.

His mind began to drift, and he found himself lost in thoughts of Jessica. He couldn't help but wonder what it would be like to make love to her in this new, elevated state of awareness. He missed their early-morning wrestling between the sheets. He yearned for the carnal ecstasy he had known with her.

A jolt of pain struck him as he realized once again that she was gone forever. He didn't try to escape the pain. In the mountains, he had learned to go deep into his pain, to experience it fully. The silence and solitude of those years had taught him to try to fully experience everything.

Daniel sat with the memory of his wife, and an overwhelming sadness rose in him. He sat with it for hours, allowing it to wash over him like waves washing over the beach.

When he surfaced from the meditation, his thoughts returned to the day he had just experienced and the days that lay ahead.

It had been an eventful day, and Daniel quickly realized there would need to be some guidelines for visitors. So, taking a small piece of cardboard, he wrote the following:

WELCOME.
*To help make this a fruitful experience for as many people as possible, we ask that you follow these guidelines:*
*1. One visitor on the porch at a time.*
*2. I need a few moments between each visit to refocus. I may close my eyes; that doesn't mean I'm asleep (though if I start snoring, that probably means I am).*
*3. Use this time to quiet your heart and consider why you have come here.*
*4. We are all here to listen, not only with our ears, but with our whole being. You don't need to take notes. You will remember what you need to remember. If you don't remember something, that message wasn't for you.*
*5. Be gentle with one another. Every person you meet is fighting a hard battle, carrying a heavy burden, and grappling with their own questions. Be kind and generous. You know the burden you carry; it's best to assume those around you carry an even greater burden.*
*6. Be patient. The waiting is part of the experience. Impatience is a thief that will rob you of the fullness of this experience.*

*Daniel*

The next morning, Daniel asked Sean to give the card to the first person in line, and to have her pass it down the line.

## 25. SUNDAY MORNING

On Sunday morning, Daniel woke, had a light breakfast, showered, shaved, and dressed. Looking out the window from his bedroom, he saw the crowds and was moved with compassion. They seemed lost and confused but hopeful, and he felt the burden of their hope.

He walked out the back door and down the lane behind the house, toward the town square. Someone saw him crossing the square and walking into the church, and word spread quickly. Some people, afraid of losing their place, stayed in line in front of his house. Others put something down to hold their place and followed Daniel into town.

Daniel did this every Sunday, and within three weeks, the Fire Chief came to see the Pastor. "You can't have this many people in the church at one time," he explained.

"I understand," the Pastor replied. "How do you suggest I handle this situation?"

"I'm not sure there is anything you can do about it," the Fire Chief explained, "but it's my job to come down here and tell you what I have told you. So, I've done my job, and I suggest you keep doing yours."

The Pastor smiled.

"I am, however, going to send someone on my team down here each Sunday. To ensure everyone stays safe," the Fire Chief continued.

"We'd appreciate that," the Pastor replied.

The Pastor looked at the Fire Chief, and the Fire Chief looked at the Pastor. "It's the strangest thing, isn't it?"

"Yes and no," the Pastor replied. "Throughout history, God has always sent prophets to remind people of what matters most, to help people rearrange their priorities and refocus their lives."

The two men stood quietly for a moment, heads down in thought, and then the Pastor continued. "Daniel is clearly doing a lot of good for a lot of people. And he shows up here every Sunday, so he isn't confused about who he is and who he isn't."

"You're right," the Fire Chief said, rubbing his hand across his face. "I just worry."

"If you want to worry about anyone," the Pastor replied, "I would say worry about Daniel. It's an enormous responsibility to carry, and the truth is, humanity has a horrible track record for how we have treated people like him."

The Fire Chief considered what the Pastor said. "You're right. I hadn't thought of it that way. Thank you, Pastor. I'm glad I stopped by." He turned to leave, but after five or six steps, he paused and turned back toward the Pastor. "Has it changed you in any way?"

The Pastor smiled somberly. "I'm ashamed to admit it, but the larger the crowds get, the more time I spend preparing my Sunday message."

"I suppose that's only human," the Chief said as the men parted ways.

## 26. ONE MAN'S TRASH

Javier was driving home from the hospital one night when something beckoned him toward Daniel's place. It was late, but he decided to stop by and see if Daniel was still awake.

The living room light was on in the front of the house, so he parked and made his way to the front door. As he went to knock, the door opened. Daniel was standing there and said, "Javier, so good to see you. I was thinking about you not more than thirty minutes ago."

Javier wondered silently if that was what had beckoned him to Daniel's place so late.

"Welcome. Would you like something to drink? Water? A glass of wine?" Daniel asked.

"No thanks, I'm fine," Javier replied.

"Are you sure?" Daniel pressed.

"Okay, sure, I'll have a glass of wine."

"Red or white?"

"Red, please."

Daniel went to the kitchen and poured a glass of wine. Returning to the living room he handed it to Javier and asked, "What's new in your world?"

"Not much. Working a lot."

"What's the best thing that happened today?" Daniel asked, trying to draw his friend out.

Javier didn't respond, but Daniel could tell he was thinking. The old friends were comfortable in each other's presence, and that made Daniel happy.

"I treated a little girl today," Javier said after a while. "She had fallen and had a huge gash on her head, but she was still so full of joy. She had been having so much fun playing with her friends, and the whole time I was treating her, she talked about all the things they had done before she hurt herself. It was as if the injury was only a footnote."

"How old was she?" Daniel asked.

"Five."

Daniel smiled and thought of his daughters. He missed them. Everything reminded him of them, and he still mourned the unlived moments of their lives. Moments they would never get to experience, moments he would never get to share with his girls.

Javier knew what Daniel was thinking, but he asked anyway. "What are you thinking, my friend?"

"Not what, who. Never what, always who. The girls," Daniel replied disjointedly with pain in his voice. "When they were little, every day was their first something. Their first word. The first time they said, 'Mom.' The first time they smiled. The first time they crawled, and stood up, and walked. Their first day at school . . . every time I turned around, they were having a first. It made life magical."

Javier sat listening. He didn't know what to say. He was afraid that he would say the wrong thing and trigger a deep sadness in his friend.

The two men sat quietly for a long time, but it wasn't awkward or uncomfortable. It was the well-worn ability of two people to simply be together.

"Did you have something you wanted to ask me, Javier?" Daniel asked, breaking the silence.

"How did you know?"

"Just a sense."

"It's nothing, really," Javier said, shaking his head. "Sort of a weird question, but I can't seem to get it out of my mind. The story about the girl you healed in the mountains. I have heard several people retell it, and each time they mentioned that you gave her some chocolate."

Daniel laughed. He had been expecting a piercing question from the sharp mind of his lifelong friend. Amid his laughter, he said, "That's right. I gave her some chocolate. Sean jokes that it was the chocolate that cured her."

"I warned you: it's a weird question. Where did you get the chocolate?"

Daniel laughed again. "Great question. Here I was, thinking you had a deep question you wanted to discuss, but no, it's about the chocolate."

"Sorry . . ." Javier began, but Daniel gently stopped him.

"No need to apologize, my friend. You know I'm kidding. It's a great question. I'm surprised nobody has asked before now. The chocolate was left behind by hikers. It's amazing all the things people leave up there.

"Waste and entitlement were two of the early lessons the mountains taught me. It quickly became apparent that I had been living a life of excess and waste. We need so little, and yet we complicate our lives with so much. I learned that I could live like a king with the things other people threw away. What one person considers worthless or inconvenient can literally be life-sustaining to another person. People were discarding almost everything I needed to live. One man's trash truly is another man's treasure.

"It is written: 'Live simply so that other people may simply live.'

"There is great wisdom in this saying, but like most truths, it challenges us to abandon comfort for a more authentic path."

The two old friends stayed up late talking. This had been a cornerstone of their friendship since high school. Their late-night discussions were epic. Javier was happy to have his old friend back, and Daniel delighted in the normalcy of the situation. By the time Daniel went to sleep, it was almost time to get up again.

## 27. THE BRUTAL TRUTH

The following day seemed endless to Daniel. This was unusual. He didn't know why, exactly. He wasn't tired, just a little restless. So, when Sean came up and said the next visitor would be his last for the day, Daniel felt a faint sense of relief.

A moment later, a young man in his early thirties stepped onto the porch and settled into the rocking chair beside Daniel. He seemed confident, but Daniel sensed that all was not as it appeared.

"How may I help you?" Daniel asked.

"While I was waiting to see you, I was talking to others who have traveled from near and far. And I came to the realization that many of your visitors have come here with painful problems and pressing questions. I don't have any of those. Life is good. I have a great job, and a fabulous girlfriend, I'm healthy, my family is supportive, and I have many friends and interests.

"Still, I sense something is missing, something I can't see. They say you are a prophet. I don't know if that is true, but I'm curious what advice you'd have for someone like me."

Daniel closed his eyes. Nobody knew what he was doing when he closed his eyes. Nobody had ever asked. Sometimes he closed his eyes for a minute, and sometimes he closed them for ten. But when he finally opened them, he seemed to know exactly what he was going to say, and it always seemed to be exactly what the person in front of him needed to hear.

"What's your name?" Daniel asked.

"Jackson," the young man replied.

"I want to share two things with you. The first may seem harsh, but if you are going to find what you seek, if you are going to grow, you need to hear it."

"Okay," Jackson said, his confidence wavering.

"You make it sound like everything in your life is fine, but you and I both know that isn't true."

"What do you mean?" Jackson asked defensively.

"Well, none of the things you mentioned are going as well as you described," Daniel replied, to Jackson's surprise. "It's true you have a great job, but it's not a great job for you. The money is good, but you are not happy at work, because you know it isn't right for you. You look at the guys who are ten years older than you and can't imagine doing this for another ten years. And yet the idea of a career change fills you with a paralyzing fear.

"Your fabulous girlfriend cheated on you last year, and you keep wondering how and why it happened. But the two of you can't really talk about it, which leaves you wondering if it will happen again.

"Your father has always preferred your older brother, and your mother has never tried to understand you. You have lots of interests, but you've been steadily losing interest in them since you graduated college, and that scares you.

"You have a small group of close friends, but there are things you can't talk to them about. There are things you don't feel like you can talk to anyone about, and that leaves you feeling desperately alone. And last month you had that health scare, and while you are fine, it's the first time you've had a brush with your mortality, and that has you rattled too."

Jackson looked at Daniel, dumbfounded. "How do you know all that stuff?" he asked indignantly.

Daniel didn't answer the question. "How I know what I know is irrelevant. What is of great importance is why you refuse to confront the truth of your life. Being honest about where you are is the first essential step on the journey to where you wish to go."

"What's the second thing?" Jackson asked dismissively.

"There is no need to be embarrassed, Jackson," Daniel said, leaning in. "We all have to confront the truth about our lives. When you sat down, you said you weren't like the other people who come to see me because you don't have pressing problems or painful questions. The truth is, you have more questions and problems than most of the people who come here. But unlike my other visitors, you seem unwilling to explore them. Why do you feel the need to pretend?"

Jackson shrugged, and his shoulders sagged.

Daniel paused and took a deep breath. "You asked what advice I would have for someone like you. Confront the brutal truth about yourself and your life. Expose yourself to yourself."

"How do I do that?" Jackson asked, genuinely opening himself for the first time.

"Befriend silence, stillness, and solitude. Get comfortable in your own company. And ask yourself lots of questions," Daniel advised calmly.

"What sort of questions?" the young man asked.

"What brings you joy? What are you afraid of? What's the source of your insecurity? What do you believe about your past that is keeping you from your future? When was the last time you felt fully alive? Do the things you do every day energize you? Do you have empathy for other people? What are you dissatisfied with at this time in your life? Do you allow people to really get to know you? If not, why not? Are your friends helping you become the-best-version-of-yourself? When was the last time you did something with your whole heart? What are you pretending not to know about yourself, your life, your relationships, your career, your health, your finances? What do you believe that is simply not true? What do you believe you have to do to receive love?"

Jackson just sat there, as if he were alone.

It was amazing what Daniel could tell by the way people sat on the rocking chair. Jackson's demeanor and posture had gradually shifted into a slump. He was fidgeting now, and the rocking of his chair revealed his anxiety. He wasn't the calm and confident young man he had pretended to be when he first sat down.

"How will I remember all those questions?"

"You will remember the ones you need now. Others will resurface in your life when you are ready to be completely honest in answering them," Daniel explained.

"How do I befriend silence, stillness, and solitude?" Jackson asked now.

"We will get to how in a minute; first let's discuss why. Begin with purpose in all things. Understanding purpose is the key to mastery.

"Silence and stillness allow you to connect with your truest self. They allow you to go soul deep and explore the essence of self. In this state, you become very clear about your needs, talents, and desires, and the way forward is always found at the intersection of your needs, talents, and desires. When people say they are confused about what to do, it's rarely true. They are confused about who they are or pretending to be someone they are not.

"It is impossible to habitually spend time in silence and not know yourself. Clarity emerges from silence. This is how we move from chaos to order, from confusion to clarity."

"Why does the solitude matter?" Jackson asked.

"Solitude removes the need to pretend in any way," Daniel replied. "While we are concerned with how others are perceiving us, it's impossible to discover our truest self."

The rocking chairs swayed gently back and forth now. The afternoon breeze was gathering with more strength than usual. The sky revealed dark clouds forming to the west.

"What do I *do* in the silence?"

"Excuse me a moment," Daniel said as he stood up and walked down to where Sean was speaking with some visitors. "Do you have a moment?" he asked Sean.

Sean was startled. He couldn't remember a time when Daniel had stepped down off the porch in the middle of the day.

"Of course—is everything okay?" Sean whispered nervously.

"Everything is fine, but in about fifteen minutes all these people are going to get soaked. Take them down to Ezra's and ask him to give them some coffee and sandwiches. I'll join you all there when I'm finished visiting with this young man."

Returning to his rocking chair, Daniel repeated Jackson's question: "What do you do in the silence, stillness, and solitude? You can read, but over time you will let go of that as you realize you can learn more in an hour of silence than you can in a year from books. You can meditate, reflect, and pray, but remember, we are in search of the wordless prayer. The stillness, silence, and solitude will teach you how to simply be, and once you have learned how to do that, everything you do will be infinitely more impactful.

"In time, you will discover that you don't need to do anything. This is one of life's greatest lessons: The purpose of life isn't to rush here and there mindlessly doing all manner of things, but rather to do the essential things that enable you to become all you were created to be.

"It is written: 'You do not need to leave your room. Remain sitting at your table and listen. You do not even need to listen—simply wait, be quiet, still, and solitary. The world will freely offer itself to you to be unmasked—it has no choice. It will roll in ecstasy at your feet.'"

A hopeful look passed across Jackson's face but faded quickly. Most people left Daniel feeling like a weight had been lifted, but as this young man walked away, Daniel knew he was leaving with a heavy heart. He wished there was more he could do to help, but he also knew that what needed to be done the young man could only do for himself.

## 28. LOVE

The coffee shop was more alive than ever as Daniel walked through the door. There were people everywhere. His eyes met Ezra's behind the counter, and they smiled with the uncommon joy of two men following their destinies.

Ezra motioned toward the corner, and Daniel noticed a large empty chair. As he made his way toward it, a hush came over the place. Relaxing into the big comfy chair, Daniel glanced around. The people looked at him expectantly, their eyes full of hope.

"What should we talk about?" he asked casually.

"***Speak to us about* LOVE**," an anonymous voice called out.

"Ah, yes," Daniel murmured almost imperceptibly. "Never has something so crucial to the human experience been so misunderstood.

"Love ennobles us. The very nature of love is soul-expanding. It nourishes our hearts, minds, bodies, and souls.

"Romantic love dominates the conversation in our culture. But romantic love is a poor guide to the many worlds of love and a distorted lens through which to understand the essence of love.

"The idea of falling in love endears us to the notion that love is easy and pleasurable, but what we call 'falling in love' is not love. Loving someone and being in love may collide at times, but they are not the same thing.

"Falling in love comes with feelings of forever, but feelings are unreliable and unsustainable. Any relationship based on feelings alone will therefore be unreliable and unsustainable. Feelings by their very nature are fleeting, and so any effort to make the 'in love' phenomenon last is doomed to fail. Our desire to make something last forever that will inevitably end is a delusion that leaves us unprepared for a sustainable relationship."

The people seemed to lean closer to Daniel as the conversation unfolded. The comforting aroma of coffee drifted through the air. Occasionally, the delicious scent of a fresh batch of cakes or cookies would waft over, and Daniel's mouth would water.

"Two people fall in love, but as time passes, you discover that he isn't all you thought he was, and he discovers that you aren't all he thought you were. Together you realize that you are each fragile, imperfect, wounded, and yet wonderful. In that moment, you are on the threshold of togetherness, confronted by this question: Do we want to be fragile, imperfect, wounded, and wonderful together?"

Daniel was about to continue when he sensed someone wanted to ask a question. It came from a young woman standing at the counter by the espresso machine.

"What assumptions do we make about love that limit us from experiencing it?" she asked.

"The first assumption we make is in thinking we know what love is, or even what the word *love* means, and that everyone agrees on a definition. Socrates revolutionized philosophy by beginning the discussion of each new topic with a simple question: What is it? So, let us follow in his footsteps: What is love?

"It is written: 'To love is to will the good of the other.'

"Love is by its very nature focused on the other. It isn't self-seeking. To love is to desire what is good for the other person. This has nothing to do with feelings or romance, and this realization leads us to what is common among the many types of human love. There is the love between family and friends, romantic love, and the love we have for neighbors and strangers. But the nature of love does not change. In every instance, love is to will the good of the other.

"Love is therefore a choice, an act of the will—not a feeling and not fate," Daniel continued. "It's something you do, not something that happens to you. Your decision to love may be accompanied by great feelings, but it doesn't have to be. Love is a verb, not a noun."

The crowd was ever so still now. Daniel studied the faces in the crowd, full of hope and longing. The stillness was broken by another question. Every head seemed to turn at once. He recognized the voice. It was Madison, the daughter of the local wine dealer. She was standing with some friends toward the back of the store.

"How should we choose who to spend our lives with?" Madison

asked. The gravitational force of her youth drew the conversation back to romantic love. Daniel sighed ever so faintly, smiled, and decided not to resist.

"Our deepest desire is to love and to be loved. There are obviously many factors. Physical attraction, character and values, priorities, hopes and dreams, work ethic, ease and ability to converse, willingness to commit, and sense of humor, to name a few. But the one we often overlook is the other person's ability to love. We unconsciously assume everyone's ability to love is equal, but that isn't true. Some people can run faster than others, some people are more financially astute than others, and some people can love more than others. Choose the person who can love you the most."

A silence fell over the room now. "How will we know who can love us the most?" Madison persisted.

"Our ability to love is determined by self-possession. We can love only to the extent that we are free. Someone enslaved by addiction cannot love—their whole being is focused on attending to their addiction. They have entered into a completely self-focused state.

"To will the good of another, to act for the good of another, to choose love requires the freedom of self-possession. Love is the generous gift of self. But to give ourselves, we must first possess ourselves. We can give ourselves only to the extent that we possess ourselves.

"So, be careful who you allow into your heart. Who you choose to love will raise you up or tear you down. Never pledge your love to someone with no self-control. To fall in love with someone incapable of loving you back is a life-altering tragedy, and a person with no self-control cannot love you back.

"Love can be pleasurable and easy, but if you expect that all the time, you will become disillusioned, for love is also painful and difficult. If you look to a relationship to solve your problems, you will be disappointed. Relationships don't solve problems; they bring new problems, but those problems are precious opportunities for soul expansion. The difficult and unwelcome situations of relationships also hold the solutions to the unsolved mysteries in our hearts.

"Love is a choice. Anyone can choose love when it's pleasurable and circumstances are favorable, but the person who can love you the most can also choose love amid difficult and unexpected circumstances."

"Why is love so difficult?" Madison asked now.

"It is written: 'All things excellent are as difficult as they are rare.'

"You yearn for a love that is excellent. You know by looking around at other people's relationships that the love you yearn for is rare. Everything rare is difficult. If it were easy, it would be common. All excellence requires rigor and discipline and perseverance—and that is why excellence is so rare."

Daniel noticed a young man trying to get his attention. He was standing in the group with Madison, and Daniel wondered if they were together.

"How can we expand our own capacity to love?" the young man asked. *It was a winsome question*, Daniel thought to himself.

"Every act of disciplined self-control increases your capacity to love. Take the stairs instead of the elevator. Listen patiently when you'd rather not. Help your younger brother even though it's inconvenient. Smile joyfully at those who irritate you. Have a glass of water even though you are craving soda. Approach your work with discipline. Let someone else decide what to do or where to eat. Overlook the annoying traits of the people you live and work with. Hold your tongue when your comment adds little to the conversation. Get out of bed without delay each morning. Leave the last bite of something delicious. Deny yourself in small ways so you can possess yourself completely. This is how you expand your capacity to love and be loved."

Ezra directed Daniel's attention toward another young woman who wanted to ask a question. Daniel invited her to speak, and she asked, "What else would you say to those of us venturing out into the world?"

"Give some thought to what life is really all about. Throughout your life, people will try to convince you that this or that is the most important thing. But life is only about one thing.

"It isn't about what brand of shoes you wear. It's not about what grades you get in school. Life's not about how big your house is or what street you live on. Life's not about what brand of car you drive. It's not about what football team or baseball team you support. It's not about whether your team wins. It's not about whether you made the football team, or might make the football team, or what position you had on the football team. Life's not about what college you went to, or might go to, or what college your kids are going to. Life isn't about these things. Life's not about money. It's not about power or influence. It's not about fame. It's not about where you vacation. It's not about the labels on your clothes. It's not about who you've dated or who you're dating. And it's not about who you know. Life isn't about these things.

"Life is about love. It's about how you love and hurt the people closest to you. It's about how you love and hurt yourself. It's about how you love and hurt the people who cross your path for a moment. Life is about love."

The people were quiet, calm, and still. As they sat reflecting, Madison, the daughter of the wine dealer, reentered the conversation.

"Day after day, you sit on your rocking chair visiting with people from all over the world. What do you discover in those conversations?"

Daniel smiled. He loved engaging with young people in these rigorous discussions.

"It's often the simple things we overlook that matter most in the end. Seduced by the new and complex, we condescend to the simple things that could save us from all manner of heartaches and disappointments."

"What's an example of one of these simple things as it relates to love and relationships?" Madison pressed in her youthful exuberance.

Daniel lowered his head and sighed almost imperceptibly. He knew many people would find his answer unsatisfactory.

"Kindness. So many negative scenarios are automatically avoided if two people are kind to each other. Now, think of all the questions people ask about a potential spouse, and what do we forget to ask: Is he a kind person? Does she have a kind heart? Two kind people will always have a better relationship than two inconsiderate people. All relationships come down to kindness in the end."

## 29. QUESTIONS

As Daniel stepped out onto the porch the next morning, his eyes met with those of a young woman. She was first in line and stunningly beautiful. His heart skipped a beat, and something stirred in his loins, taking him off guard. It was a stirring he had not experienced in quite some time.

Daniel sat in his rocking chair, and Sean invited his first visitor to join him on the porch. As she sat down, a butterfly with luminous lavender wings came to rest on her hand. She didn't flinch. She didn't even glance down at the butterfly. It was as if it were the most natural thing in the world, and Daniel became intrigued by her in a whole new way.

Her name was Sophia. She had long, dark brown hair that flowed gracefully around her head and shoulders. Her eyes were rich chocolate brown and deeper than the deepest well. Daniel was getting lost in her eyes as she began speaking.

"I'm not exactly sure why I came here. I have so many questions about life and myself. My friends and family tell me I think too much . . ." Sophia said, trailing off mid-sentence.

Daniel was struck by how self-assured she seemed, but he could tell she was a touch nervous too.

"Do you think most people think too much or too little?" he asked her.

Sophia sensed it was a rhetorical question. Daniel smiled, and she matched his smile.

"How do you know what to spend your days reflecting on?" she asked.

"You mentioned you have many questions about life and about yourself. Questions are a wise old teacher. Learning to listen to the questions that silently emerge in our hearts is a quintessential life skill. Your questions are the gateway to your destiny, and destiny cannot be rushed. Allow it to unfold before you and within you."

"What if the same questions keep emerging?" she asked.

"The important questions will keep emerging until we attend to them. Our lives are an intimate answer to life's biggest questions.

"It is written: 'Be patient toward all that is unsolved in your heart and try to love the questions themselves, like locked rooms and like books that are now written in a very foreign tongue. Do not now seek the answers, which cannot be given you because you would not be able to live them. And the point is to live everything. Live the questions now. Perhaps you will then gradually, without noticing it, live along some distant day into the answer.'

"Treasure your questions. Honor them with patience. It's natural to be excited, but don't try to rush to answers. Cherish them. Look around, take it all in, breathe deeply, and drink fully of the questions that are emerging in your heart. It takes courage to explore our questions, it takes patience to wait on the answers, and it takes wisdom to live the answers we receive.

"The world cannot give you the answers you seek. The people in your life cannot answer these questions for you, even those who love you most. Each question is itself an invitation to inhabit yourself in new and deeper ways. Answering these questions is soul work."

The two sat quietly, and Daniel could see Sophia's intriguing mind working.

"How do I go deeper into my questions?" she asked after a few minutes.

"We tend to think of answering questions as a mental exercise, but life's questions can only be answered with your whole self. They cannot be answered by thinking alone.

"Learn to feel your questions. When you are pondering a question, where do you feel it in your body? In your head, in your throat, your chest, heart, gut, groin? How does the question make you feel? Happy, sad, frustrated, angry, resentful, hopeful, doubtful, fearful, joyful?

"In the same way, learn to feel the answers. When we receive an answer to a question, we test it against reference points: common sense, past experiences, hopes and expectations, wisdom teachings, and our values and priorities. But our feelings are a highly intuitive evaluative function. Feel your answers. Where in your body do you feel the answer you are receiving? What emotions does that answer give rise to?

"This process can be uncomfortable. Transformation is uncomfortable. Life is full of mystery, and learning to enjoy the uncertainty of our unanswered questions is the beginning of wisdom."

"You've thought a lot about this, haven't you?" Sophia asked.

Daniel smiled. "Yes. Questions are one of the most consequential realities of our lives. When I first went to the mountains, my mind was full of toxic thoughts and ideas. Even my questions were poisoned. But as time passed, I began to listen to the deeper questions surfacing in my heart. Some of them had been there my whole life, and I had been ignoring them. Others were new and fresh.

"Now I sit here every day and listen to other people's questions. They come here looking for answers, and I often disappoint them, because it's not my mission to provide easy answers to difficult questions. All I can do is show them how they can find their own answers."

The two fell silent again. The only sounds in the air were the gentle rocking of the two chairs, back and forth, and the chirping of the birds sitting on the telephone wires. Daniel was in no rush for Sophia to leave, but he sensed that Sean was ready to keep things moving.

"Would you like to talk about the question that is dominating your heart?" Daniel asked.

"What do you mean?" Sophia asked, suddenly self-conscious.

"We all have many questions, but at any given moment in our journey, in my experience, we are grappling with one question that is set apart from all the others."

Sophia felt emotionally naked. It was as though a veil had been removed between them. Daniel's intuition was correct. She did have such a question, but she had been trying to explore it with a general conversation. Daniel was inviting her to have a more intimate conversation, and she became hesitant. She wondered why she had started to feel that way after being so comfortable in his presence at first.

"I think the man I'm dating is about to ask me to marry him," she confessed. "We have only been dating for five months, and I'm not ready to decide if he's the person I want to build a life with."

Daniel's heart was seized with envy. It took him a moment to recognize the feeling. He couldn't remember the last time he had been envious. He wanted Sophia for himself, though he had been unconscious of it until now. At that moment, he became momentarily submerged in the dark side of his gift. He knew he could steer her away from this man, but he knew that was not his role. Daniel believed it was a spiritual crime to rob someone of her one true path—but *was* it her one true path?

He stalled to recover his composure by asking Sophia, "When you think about this situation, what question forms in your mind, and what question emerges from your heart? It may be that both questions are the same, but sometimes they are two very different questions."

"My mind fills with the many voices of family and friends. 'What's wrong with her?' is the question that floats to the surface from all that chatter, and I know that's the wrong question. My heart says . . . well, now that I think about it, I'm not sure what question my heart is asking," she said quietly, a little lost in her thoughts.

"What do you think that tells you?" Daniel asked.

"I'm not sure," Sophia said wistfully. The conversation had shifted. Sadness had suddenly shown its face. They seemed to be daydreaming in tandem. A minute or two passed before she asked, "If you had to summarize our conversation about questions with one idea, what would it be?"

*Her questions are different*, Daniel thought. *They are brilliant and intriguing.*

"One idea," he said quietly, as if talking to himself, and then paused before saying, "Love your questions, and they will love you back."

Sophia smiled. She was deeply touched. Daniel's life had become so integrated that he could effortlessly distill the wisdom of a conversation into a single sentence. It was a beautiful sentence, a beautiful idea: Love your questions, and they will love you back.

"Thank you," she said as she stood. He stood with her. "I've taken up too much of your time, but I very much enjoyed our time together." She reached out and shook his hand. Her hands were as smooth as silk, perhaps the softest Daniel had ever held.

"It was a pleasure to meet you," he said, not wanting to let go of her hand, and then she left.

As Sophia walked away, Daniel ached. Something in him wanted to go after her, to invite her for coffee. He realized he was watching her, and then he realized Sean was watching him watching her. Sean smiled at him, and Daniel became self-conscious. It was another unfamiliar feeling.

Sitting back down on his rocking chair, Daniel closed his eyes, hoping, dreaming, praying that their paths would cross again. Then he smiled a deep, satisfying smile. It had been a long time since he had asked something for himself.

## 30. THE CHILL OF DESTINY

Sophia strolled into town. The square was full of life. Children were running and playing. Adults sat on the benches, talking and reading. She sat down on one of the iconic park benches that had become a symbol of the town. At the other end sat a woman in her sixties. It was Ezra's wife, Leah.

"Hello," Leah said in a tone that was warm and joyful.

"Hi," Sophia replied.

"Are you visiting?" Leah inquired to be friendly, though she knew the answer.

"Yes, I arrived a couple of days ago. I was first in line to visit with him this morning."

"How did it go?" Leah asked.

"Amazing. I don't know how long I was in that rocking chair, but for that time, he made me feel as if I was the only other person in the world," Sophia shared, her eyes glazed with the memory.

Leah smiled. "Yes, he has that effect on people."

"He's a very special man, isn't he?" Sophia asked.

"Yes, he really is. The world could use a few more just like him."

"Do you know him?" Sophia asked now, turning toward Leah.

"I do. But my husband knows him much better than I do."

"How do people think of him here in town?" Sophia asked, letting her curiosity get the better of her and inching closer to Leah.

"Everyone thinks of him in their own way, but I have noticed that what people think of him usually says more about them than it does about him," Leah replied.

*Profound*, Sophia thought, and admiration for Leah continued to swell in her heart. "How do *you* think of him?" she pressed gently.

"Ezra and I were talking about this the other night. Ezra is my husband," Leah explained. "People have given Daniel so many names, and I do believe he's a prophet, but for some reason, I think of him as a philosopher. A wise man. A lover of wisdom."

Sophia felt a flutter of hope in her heart, and all the blood in her body seemed to rush to her face. *Lover of Sophia*, she thought, as her cheeks reddened. *I wish.*

"You're blushing, my girl. What did I say?" Leah asked.

"Philosopher. Lover of wisdom. Philo-Sophia," Sophia murmured wistfully.

"Why did that make you blush?" Leah inquired, perplexed.

"My name is Sophia."

"Oh my!" Leah exclaimed.

"I suppose every woman falls in love with him a little," Sophia observed.

Leah smiled. "Yes, but as you were speaking, I felt the chill of destiny go through me."

# 31. LOVE REKINDLED

Weeks turned into months, and the town found a new routine. Some people were elated that Daniel was there. Others were not. Stories about him spread across the country and around the world. The media was a constant presence, even though Daniel refused to do interviews, and hundreds of people visited every day now. They came looking for an answer to a question, they came desperate for healing, and they came simply out of curiosity.

Ezra couldn't bake his cakes and cookies fast enough. His whole being radiated joy. "Oh, Daniel, what a coward I was to ignore my dream all these years! I'm a new man," he said to Daniel one day.

Leah was having a late breakfast with her girlfriends, and they commented to her, "Ezra looks amazing. What is he doing? Eating differently? Exercising? He seems so happy."

"It's true," Leah agreed, smiling. "It's amazing how chasing a dream changes a man. I've known the man for almost fifty years, and I have never seen him happier. He has never had more energy, and he's so attentive to me."

"What do you mean?" her girlfriends probed.

Leah blushed, and the women leaned closer. "All right, all right. I'll tell you, but only if you promise not to tell anyone. Ever."

"We swear, Leah—tell us!" her friends exclaimed, intrigued to hear what she had to say. They just knew this was going to be good.

"Ezra will be seventy years old next month, and our lovemaking is better than ever before. I mean, when we got married, we were both so young, and it was fabulous, and then came our 'sexual prime' according to the experts, and that was great too. But something has been unleashed in him that I have never seen before . . . and I like it."

Her friends gaped at her, speechless.

"Anyway, I must go," Leah said casually and with a mischievous smile. "Ezra is coming home for lunch, and I want to make sure he has *everything* he needs." Then she stood up, kissed her girlfriends goodbye, and was gone.

The other women sat there, stunned, looking at one another. In all the years they had known Leah, they had never heard her even mention that topic. Never. Not once.

Becca finally broke the silence. "Well, good for her!" and they all laughed.

## 32. WORSHIPPING EFFICIENCY

As the sun was rising the following morning, Sean was sitting in the kitchen drinking coffee, waiting for Daniel earlier than usual. Something had been bothering him for a couple of weeks now.

"Good morning, Sean."

"Morning, Daniel."

"You're early. Is everything okay?"

"Can I ask you a question?" Sean replied.

"Anything."

"I'm concerned that people are having to wait too long, and I wondered if you'd consider spending less time with each person," Sean ventured cautiously.

Daniel sat quietly pondering what Sean had said for a moment. Sean had grown accustomed to this and simply waited.

"You are a good man, Sean," Daniel said, affirming him. "Your care and concern for the people who come to visit is pure, but we need to remember there is no 'efficient' way to do this. Life is messy and people are messy.

"The reason I spend so much time with each person is because I need to know their hearts before I can speak into their lives. Until I know something about their pain and joy, I don't feel like I have the right to say anything.

"It is written: 'You never really understand a person until you consider things from his or her point of view.'"

"I feel bad for the people waiting," Sean explained.

"I understand," Daniel replied, "but there is no need to feel that way. The waiting is part of the experience. They live busy lives in a noisy world, and it's good for them to have an opportunity to slow down and reflect.

"You and I are children of a culture of efficiency. We've spent our lives trying to do things faster. Many things can and should be more efficient, but some things should never be made efficient. Friendship and parenting aren't efficient. Love itself isn't efficient. Relationships thrive on carefree timelessness—time together without an agenda. When we throw off the constraints of schedules and agendas, we bond in unimaginable ways. If we try to make this efficient, it will become inauthentic and inhumane," Daniel concluded.

Sean noticed something different about the tone of Daniel's voice. He couldn't pinpoint it at first, but looking up from his coffee, he met Daniel's eyes. "You seem especially passionate about this, Daniel," Sean said.

"I am."

"Why?" Sean volleyed reflexively. "I mean, I understand the reasons you've shared, but is there something more?"

"There is," Daniel replied cryptically.

Sean didn't press him. He just waited. He knew if he waited patiently, Daniel would share what was on his heart.

"You asked me once if I was afraid of anything," Daniel began. "I'm afraid of being dehumanized, of not being seen as a living, breathing person. This is one of the reasons I have never liked being called the hermit or the healer or the prophet, because these names are so impersonal.

"For years now, I have reflected long and hard on the problems we face as a civilization. The conclusion I have reached is that our best chance of preventing almost every type of suffering on this planet is to embrace a radical effort to rehumanize society. This may sound complicated, but it's actually exquisitely simple. All it requires is that we return to treating people like people. If we treat each person like the incredibly unique human being he or she is, hatred, violence, and indifference become impossible.

"Most of the problems our visitors are wrestling with have been caused by dehumanization. They have been dehumanized by others, or they are dehumanizing themselves and not even aware of it! The poverty of our culture is on full display each time people experience something that leads them to conclude, 'I don't feel treated like a human being.'

"Listening to people is a practical way to contribute to their rehumanization. When we listen to each other, we are essentially saying, 'You are a unique human being of infinite value. You matter. I'm interested in you as a person, not only because of what you can do for me.' Listening intently to each other takes us beyond the often transactional nature of modern relationships and helps us to form life-giving human connections.

"By spending as much time with each person as needed, I'm doing my small part to set in motion this great rehumanization. You are doing your part by treating each person with respect and dignity.

"Our goal isn't to meet with as many people as possible as quickly as possible. That would be dehumanizing for everyone: you, me, and our visitors. It takes as long as it takes. Those waiting can take comfort that when it's their turn, they will be treated with the same respect as each person who has gone before them."

Sean sat reflecting on what Daniel had shared. He never ceased to be amazed by his clarity and wisdom. Daniel sat drinking his coffee, eating a slice of toast, and wondering what was in store for him today.

## 33. A FATHER'S CONCERN

While Daniel sat in his kitchen imagining the day ahead, his father was walking into Ezra's for a coffee. The two old friends sat in their favorite corner and got to talking.

"It's interesting, Ezra," Daniel's father commented. "It was only a few months ago they were calling him a dangerous vagrant, and now they honor him as a great healer and modern-day prophet."

"Yes," Ezra replied. "We fear what we don't understand, and when we don't understand something, we rush to label it."

"Exactly," Daniel's father affirmed.

"You seem worried," Ezra said to his old friend.

"I am."

"About what?" Ezra inquired.

"His mother is worried about his safety. I'm worried that he's being built up to be torn down. People seem to take pleasure in both the rise and fall of others. Today he's a prophet—who knows what they'll be calling him next week?"

"Hmm," Ezra murmured knowingly, and the two men sat as customers came and went.

"What can we do about it?" Ezra finally asked.

"Very little, I'm afraid. He is following the summons of his soul, and no good father would interfere with that."

## 34. OLD SELF AND NEW SELF

It was summer again, and the days were hotter and longer than ever. And the people kept coming. Daniel sat on his rocking chair, disinterested in the world around him, completely absorbed in the person on the other rocker, whoever that was.

Each day he visited with people from sunrise to sunset. Sean and Ezra worried that he was pushing himself too hard, though he never got sick and rarely seemed tired.

"I wish he would eat more," Ezra said to Sean.

"From the very beginning, I've tried to get him to break for lunch, but he won't," Sean replied. "Once he said, 'It's okay, Sean, but perhaps you could bring me one of Ezra's oatmeal raisin cookies from the kitchen.' So now, I bring him cookies and a glass of lemonade each day around noon and set them on the small table by his rocking chair. Some days he eats them, but most days he doesn't."

Before Daniel went to bed one night, he gazed out his window at all the people sleeping in his front yard. More people came every day. Some stayed at the hotel, but many camped on his lawn.

His old self would have been in a hurry to speak to them all. His old self would have stayed up all night visiting with them. His new self understood that the waiting helped prepare them. His new self also knew that staying up all night to visit with people wasn't sustainable.

Most of all, he was aware that he had been given a gift and was responsible for protecting it. This meant honoring his own humanity and taking care of his legitimate needs. This, he knew, was the secret to serving powerfully while maintaining joy.

Looking over the crowd, he whispered a prayer for these people who had come from so many places with hearts full of hope and longing. Then Daniel lay down and went to sleep.

## 35. DEEPLY PERSONAL QUESTIONS

The days turned to weeks, and the seasons came and went. In the winter, Daniel sat on the rocking chair with blankets loosely wrapped around his shoulders. Sean insisted on the blankets, and Daniel had stopped resisting the care of those around him. He didn't like the fussing, but he had learned to surrender and receive graciously.

The people came and went, each with a unique story. Every person came looking for deeply personal answers to their deeply personal questions. And yet, themes emerged, and so many people's struggles were similar.

"Does my husband still love me?"

"How am I going to dig myself out of this debt?"

"I have cancer."

"I lost my job two weeks ago, but I don't know how to tell my spouse."

"My daughter refuses to talk to me."

"Should I go back to college?"

"I feel lost."

"I'm addicted to prescription medication."

"Should I marry him?"

"I'm so unhappy at work, but can someone my age change careers?"

"I'm sick. Very sick. But I haven't told my family."

"How can I be a better father?"

"I'm worried about my grandchildren."

"I desperately want to have a baby, but we cannot seem to get pregnant."

"I think my wife is having an affair."

"I lost my job six months ago and now people treat me like a leper. They don't know what to say to me, so they avoid me."

"How do I reconcile with my son?"

"I was sexually abused as a child, and now I can't let anyone get close."

"I have a great opportunity, but it would require us to move, and my husband won't even consider it."

"I'm spiraling into an ever-deeper depression."

"I buried my child last week, and I don't think I'll ever recover."

"I'm so lonely."

"I don't know what to do with my life. I have a great job, but I'm not fulfilled. I'm too young to be this unhappy."

"I'm anxious all the time."

"Nothing makes sense anymore."

Daniel's heart ached for each person who sat in the rocking chair next to him. He had learned early on that each and every person in this world is carrying a heavy burden. But people don't carry a sign that announces their burden.

This discovery had stretched the horizons of his kindness, gentleness, and empathy. He knew if he could give people nothing else, he could at least give them these.

"What would you say most people come here looking for, Daniel?" his father asked him one night.

"Most people are simply trying to make sense of life, Dad. Their lives aren't working, and they inherently know that, but they don't know what to do about it," he replied. "They focus on the single biggest burden they are carrying, but most of the time these burdens are symptoms of the underlying dysfunction of their lives and society."

And while Daniel knew these problems were very real and caused people great stress and suffering, he was also vividly aware that those most in need were not able to visit him. This bothered him.

Still, he knew he was doing what he was called to do, where he was called to do it, for now. And he didn't take for granted that many people pass through this world and never feel that way for a single day.

## 36. AMBITION'S PRISONER

Daniel opened his eyes to speak to his next visitor and saw Melissa Mayer, the journalist, was sitting in the other rocking chair. He smiled at her warmly, and it was clear that this made her uncomfortable. He wasn't surprised to see her. He knew she would come sooner or later.

"I'm sorry," she said awkwardly but without pretense.

"For what?" Daniel asked.

"Everything."

Daniel sensed she was genuinely remorseful and that she was suffering from a guilt-ridden anguish.

"I feel horrible about what I did to you," Melissa continued.

"Was it your intention to harm me?" Daniel asked.

"No."

"What do you think was driving you?"

"Ambition," she confessed with surprising awareness and honesty. She went on to explain, "I was so hungry to succeed. Something inside me knew this was a once-in-a-generation story. Some of my instincts were spot-on, but others were way off."

"It's okay, Melissa. Be mindful that your guilt is useless unless you allow it to evolve into something more meaningful."

"I'm not sure I understand," she responded.

Now it was Melissa Mayer's turn to be surprised. Daniel's directness was piercing.

"Guilt tends to seek punishment," he explained.

"Why?" she asked.

"We yearn to make amends for our wrongdoing."

"Ahh," she sighed knowingly.

"You sense that you've done something wrong and are experiencing guilt as a result. You've been carrying the burden of that guilt for quite some time, and you came here to make amends.

"Guilt is always a crossroad. It can be a gateway to consciousness, or we can obsess over what we have done, wallow in our guilt, use it as an excuse not to grow, and fixate on the idea that we deserve punishment, rather than seeing our guilt as a signpost pointing us toward the true path."

"What does guilt direct us toward?" she asked.

"When guilt evolves into remorse, questions begin to arise. What does this mean? Why has this happened? What lesson is here for me? How are these events beckoning me to live differently? These questions are an invitation to real progress."

Time passed before Melissa asked what her shame needed to know.

"Are you angry at me?"

"No, I'm not angry at you," Daniel said, shaking his head sympathetically. "But even if I was, it doesn't matter. Your guilt is asking that question. Your guilt may even want me to be angry because it would rather be punished than take the other path. Punishment is easier than transformation."

Melissa nodded fervently. She knew Daniel was right. He was describing exactly what had been happening in her heart.

"I knew what you were doing and why you were doing it," Daniel continued. "I may have been more conscious of what you were doing than you were. I was able to see it because I did things in the service of ambition when I was working on Wall Street. I know what it's like to be ambition's prisoner. What we forget is that ambition is a form of aggression, and so, unless we are mindful of that, people will get hurt."

He paused before continuing.

"Things happen for a reason, Melissa. Sometimes it takes years, even decades, for those reasons to be revealed. I needed to come down from the mountains. It was time. If you hadn't reported the story, I may have stayed in the mountains for several more years. I may have stayed up there forever, and that wasn't my destiny. I knew that at the time, and I know it now."

"How can you be so gentle and understanding?" she asked, baffled, with tears welling.

"Acceptance of others is born of self-knowledge. I know what I have done, I know what I have failed to do, and I know what I'm capable of doing if circumstances conspire to trigger the darkness within me. Knowing these truths about myself banishes judgment and gives birth to compassion, gentleness, and understanding."

"Thank you," Melissa said with great feeling.

"You are very welcome. Be gentle with yourself. We are much more fragile than we realize."

She began to get up to leave, and Daniel said, "Aren't you forgetting something?"

"What do you mean?" Melissa asked, surprised by the question.

"Wasn't there something else you wanted to ask me?"

"There was. But I can't. It doesn't seem right after all I put you through."

"That is your guilt preferring punishment over transformation again," Daniel reminded her.

"How did you know I wanted to ask you something else?" Melissa asked.

"I had a dream about your visit."

Melissa was taken aback. It took her a moment to gather her thoughts. She looked at Daniel, then down at the ground, then off toward the mountains on the horizon. Her lower lip trembled as she began to speak. "My husband and I would very much like to have a baby, but . . ."

She began to cry. "It's going to be okay," Daniel assured her as he leaned forward in his chair, taking both of her hands in his. They

THE ROCKING CHAIR PROPHET ❋ 87

were sitting knee-to-knee now, and he whispered, "Close your eyes." She did, and he continued, "Go home tonight and make love to your husband as if it were the first time, the last time, the only time." Then he closed his eyes and began to mumble ever so faintly.

When he finished, Daniel squeezed her hands almost imperceptibly, stood up, and smiled at her. He didn't say anything else, and neither did Melissa. She made her way down the steps, and as she walked past Sean she seemed to be in a trance.

## 37. THE ANSWERS ARE WITHIN

It was late on Tuesday night when Daniel finished meeting with people. He walked in the front door, through the house, and straight out the back door. Crossing the backyard, he slipped out the gate, and walked down the lane toward the town square.

From a distance, he saw a light on in Ezra's coffee shop. It seemed late for anyone to be there.

Peering through the window, he saw Leah and Ezra at the back of the store and tapped gently on the glass. They both turned and smiled in unison.

"How are you, my friend?" Ezra said, beaming, as he opened the door.

"I'm good, thank you," Daniel responded. "You're here late."

"I was leaving," Leah said as she kissed Daniel gently on the cheek.

Daniel smiled as he surveyed the shop. "This place looks amazing, Ezra. You must be very proud."

"I don't know about proud, but I am working harder than ever, I'm happier than ever, I'm more fulfilled than I ever thought possible, and I'm very, very grateful."

"I'm glad, my friend, I'm glad," Daniel said thoughtfully.

"Are you hungry?" Ezra asked.

Daniel was about to say no out of habit when he caught himself. "Actually, I am a little hungry, Ezra. The aroma of the baking must have stirred my appetite."

"Come, let me feed you," Ezra said, waving Daniel toward the kitchen. "I'll sit with you while you eat, and we can visit."

"Very well," Daniel said.

Ezra made him a sandwich—avocado, tomato, and sprouts—then he cut Daniel a slice of caramel apple cake, and the two men sat in Ezra's favorite corner. They talked about old times, and they talked about how things had changed. Ezra wondered how Daniel was doing with his new life, and Daniel shared that in some ways, this was the most satisfying time of his life. Ezra knew Daniel's word choice held the shadow of his departed wife and daughters.

After Daniel had eaten and Ezra had finished his glass of wine, the two men sat quietly, letting time pass unnoticed. They were so comfortable in each other's company that neither felt the need to speak.

It was Ezra who finally broke the silence. "Daniel, can I ask you a question about the work you do with the people who come to visit?"

"Of course, anything."

"I've heard you say many times that the answers people seek are already within them. But if that is true, why do they come to see you? I mean, people come all this way—some travel thousands of miles, wait for hours or days, and then you tell them the answers are already within them?" Ezra asked, puzzled by the irony.

A wisp of sadness crossed Daniel's face. It was ever so slight. Someone who didn't know him wouldn't have perceived it.

"It's because they have never been taught to sit alone in the classroom of silence and listen to the gentle voice within," Daniel explained. "They have never been taught to affirm their immense capacity for good, and as a result, they lack the courage to pursue their destinies."

"Is this inner voice your conscience?" Ezra inquired, shifting closer.

"It is that, and it is so much more than that," Daniel continued. "It's also the voice of profound consciousness. It's the very best version of yourself talking to you. It is the voice of the Divine Spirit within you.

"This is an astounding gift, but few are taught to embrace it. Quite the opposite, in fact. Most of us are told to ignore it in favor of other voices.

"So, by the time people come to visit me, the voice within has grown so faint, and their confidence in that voice so weak, that they have lost their way. I'm a fool compared to the wisdom of their own hearts. This is why whatever insight I share with them is simply to help reorient their lives while they learn to listen to the gentle voice within again."

Daniel could tell that Ezra's curiosity had not been fully satisfied. "Let me ask you a question, my friend."

"Anything!" Ezra agreed.

"As you look back on your life, do you have regrets?"

Ezra's face fell ever so slightly, his shoulders curled, and he exhaled a long and labored sigh. "Yes. A few. More than I ever thought I would. Some I have made peace with, but others I still find myself ruminating upon when I'm tired and alone."

"Ponder another question with me," Daniel said. "Are these regrets the result of listening to the voice within or ignoring that voice?"

Ezra went to answer and then paused, swallowing, and a moment later a tear ran down his old face and came to rest in the deepest wrinkle of his lower cheek. There was a time when Daniel would have felt self-conscious about bringing a friend to tears, but he had learned that tears can be tremendously healing.

"When I look back on my life, I see with disturbing clarity that I knew the better path in each of those situations, but I ignored the truth I possessed in my heart," Ezra confessed.

"And when you have had the courage to live your life in accordance with the voice within, have you ever regretted that?" Daniel asked.

Ezra shook his head.

"Me neither," Daniel affirmed. "We make foolish choices, and we make excuses, but we never pause to recognize that all of life's regrets are born from ignoring the gentle voice within."

"How did you learn to listen to your inner voice?" Ezra asked.

"Well, it's important to remember that when we were young, we heard it clearly, allowed it to guide us, and experienced unmitigated joy.

"But the world is full of voices, and as time passes, we begin to ignore the voice within. The more we question it, doubt it, and ignore it, the fainter it grows—until one day it becomes so faint that we have to strain to hear it at all.

"We spend the rest of our lives trying to reclaim that gentle voice."

"So, we don't need to be taught so much as we need to be encouraged to tune into it again?" Ezra asked.

"Exactly. My father championed this. When I was a child, whenever I would ask him if I could do something or buy something, he would ask, 'What is the voice within you saying?' I hated that question at the time, but this is how I learned one of life's quintessential lessons. And even as an adult, when I would turn to him for advice, the first thing he'd say was, 'What is the voice within you saying?'

"As I grew older, I stopped listening to my father. I started paying too much attention to all the other voices in this world. I stopped listening to the voice within, made a lot of mistakes, and as a result, I hurt people, and I hurt myself."

"Were there other people who encouraged you to listen to that voice?" Ezra asked now.

"Sure, teachers and coaches, and my mother, of course. And from time to time, I would end up on the rocking chair next to Charlie. I realize now that I went to Charlie looking for answers the same way people come to me now. He would say, 'What's your heart saying to you, kid?' That aggravated me too. There were times I walked off that porch so angry and resentful, especially when I was a teenager, because I knew *he knew* what I should do, but he wouldn't tell me."

Ezra was fascinated. He had never heard Daniel speak of these things. They were like missing jigsaw pieces helping Ezra to understand how Daniel had become the man before him today.

"My time on Wall Street didn't help. I quickly became mesmerized by shiny things and addicted to external affirmation, and that allowed me to be seduced and manipulated by so many people in so many ways. But providence brought Jessica into my life, and her presence helped reorient me."

A look came over Daniel's face. Ezra had seen it before. It was a combination of reminiscing, longing, and anguish.

A lingering moment passed before Daniel spoke again. His face was racked with pain. "My God, I miss my wife," he whispered as he began to weep quietly. It was like a cry for help from the Book of Psalms. Ezra moved his chair closer, put his arm around Daniel, and let him weep into his shoulder.

When Daniel finished crying, he didn't apologize, nor did he seem embarrassed or self-conscious in any way.

"Then I went into the mountains," Daniel continued. "There were no distractions up there. For the first time in my life, I found myself inescapably face-to-face with myself. For the first few months, I was filled with self-pity and rage.

"The pain was unlike anything I had ever experienced. It went far beyond physical pain. It went beyond mental anguish. My soul literally hurt. It was soul pain.

"Time passed, and the pain began to give way to a soul-wrenching sadness. I was so disoriented that I didn't know if I preferred the pain or the sadness. But it was around that time that the voice within began to reemerge with alluring clarity. It was . . . refreshing. It was like meeting myself for the first time.

"I spent hours each day sitting on a large rock beside a lake, reflecting on my life and listening to the mysteries echoing in my heart. The suffering had finally connected me with my feelings. I had done a lot of thinking my whole life, but not much feeling. I would sit and allow my feelings to float to the surface: anger, depression, fear, resentment, sadness, anxiety, loneliness, grief. As each feeling floated to the surface, I would sit with it, sometimes for days, allowing it to run its course, allowing it to wear itself out."

"When did things begin to turn around for you?" Ezra asked.

"I remember the very moment. I was sitting on that rock, and rain began to fall gently on the other end of the lake. The dark clouds were moving in my direction, and the rain gradually made its way across the lake toward me. The first drop of rain that fell on my face was like a clash of thunder. It woke me up. I thought I may have been struck by lightning. But as the rain continued to fall, I became drenched, and then . . . joy. The pure joy of the present moment. Immersed in that experience, I set aside my past and my future and allowed the moment to hold me tight. In that moment, I knew I was going to survive the crucible life had thrown me into. And it gave me something I thought I had lost forever: hope."

# 38. NOBLE SERVICE

Around lunchtime a couple of days later, Sean approached Daniel, who had closed his eyes to collect his thoughts. When he opened them, he expected to find his next visitor, but Sean was sitting across from him instead.

"It's you, Sean!" Daniel exclaimed.

"Yes, sir," he replied.

"Why do you keep calling me that? I've asked you not to."

"I know, but it's the least I can manage," Sean explained. He was famous for these non-answer answers.

"What's on your mind?" Daniel asked.

"The people here in town have so much they would like to talk to you about," the great Irishman said sheepishly, "but they feel strange waiting in line to speak to a man they have known since he was a little boy."

Daniel smiled, "What do you suggest we do?"

"Well, I've been turning it over in my mind for a few days—perhaps we could invite them here one Sunday evening for a small gathering."

"Great idea!" Daniel exclaimed, more enthusiastically than Sean was expecting. "Let's do it the Sunday after next. Who could we ask to help with the planning?"

"I'll do it," Sean said enthusiastically.

Daniel looked at his friend sympathetically. "Sean, can I ask you something?"

"Anything."

"You're here almost every day, serving the people who come to visit—why do you do it? Why have you stayed with it? What has it meant to you?"

Sean's brow furrowed as he searched for the right words. "Well, this has been a delightful time in my life. Here on your front lawn, serving your visitors, I have found the meaning and fulfillment I have been searching for my whole life."

"Why do you think that is?" Daniel inquired.

"It is written: 'The best way to find yourself is to lose yourself in service to others,'" Sean replied.

"You've been eavesdropping," Daniel joked, and both men laughed. Daniel knew that from where Sean spent his days, he could hear almost everything that was said on the porch.

"I know you could organize the gathering," Daniel continued. "But think about what you described, Sean. This is a chance to invite others to participate in that joy.

"It is written: 'Our need to give is much greater than other people's need to receive. Their need to receive is obvious; our need to give is hidden. And as desperate as their need to receive appears, our need to give is even more desperate.'"

"Understood," Sean replied. This was one of the things Daniel loved about him. He was brief and to the point.

"Perfect," Daniel said. "And thank you, Sean. This is going to be wonderful."

As he walked down the stairs, Sean smiled at Daniel's next guest, a young woman in her late twenties, but she didn't smile back. He invited her onto the porch to visit with Daniel, and as he looked closer, she seemed to be carrying the weight of the world.

Sitting down in the rocking chair next to Daniel, she began to cry.

## 39. MAKING PREPARATIONS

The next morning, Daniel was sitting in the kitchen enjoying a light breakfast when Sean arrived. He wasn't alone. With him was the town's mayor, Tony DiCarlo.

"Good to see you, Tony. How are you?" Daniel greeted him warmly.

"I'm well, thank God," Tony replied. He ended almost every sentence with "Thank God."

"We were telling stories about when you were a child, Daniel," Sean shared.

"Is that right? Any favorites?" Daniel asked.

Sean looked at Tony, and Tony began, and they volleyed stories back and forth.

"The time you put fireworks in your mailbox and destroyed your report card."

"The time you played in the mud with all your toys and your mom told you to wash them, so you decided to wash them in the toilet bowl—but you hadn't flushed the toilet. Then your mom spent a week wondering where the smell in the house was coming from."

"And the time you wanted to see what the people talking on the radio looked like, so you opened it with a screwdriver."

"Then there was the revolving door of babysitters you terrorized."

"And we were wondering . . . how many baseballs did you and Javier hit through Charlie's windows?"

When they finished with this litany of memories, Tony and Sean were grinning from ear to ear. Shaking his head, Daniel offered the men coffee and the delicious pastries Ezra had left before sunrise.

"Sean has been telling me about the gathering you're planning for the people here in town. It's very gracious of you. Thank God!" Tony commented.

"It's the people here in town who have been gracious," Daniel insisted.

"Tell us what you're thinking, Daniel. We've put together a small group of volunteers and we'll take care of everything," Tony continued.

"I was thinking that at around four o'clock that afternoon I would stop seeing visitors and we'll clear the front lawn. This would give us a couple of hours to get everything set up and prepare to welcome the townspeople at six."

"But where will the people go who are still waiting to see you at four o'clock?" Sean implored, ever mindful of the visitors in his care.

"I was hoping Tony could visit Mr. and Mrs. Langston at the hotel and confirm that Sunday is still their slowest night. Assuming that's the case, anyone on the lawn at four o'clock will be invited to stay at the hotel. I'll cover the costs."

"Wonderful! Thank God. I'll swing by the hotel first thing," Tony confirmed.

"Tony, would you do one more thing, please?" Daniel asked.

"Of course. What is it?"

"Ask Ezra to come and visit me sometime this week. It's not urgent. Please make sure he knows that. I don't want him rushing over here in the middle of his busiest time."

"Will do," Tony said, grabbing one more cookie as he stood to leave.

Daniel was excited. "It's nice to have something to look forward to," he whispered softly to himself as he made his way out to the porch and settled into his rocking chair once more.

## 40. DEPRESSION

Later that evening, as Daniel sat in the living room reading and reflecting, his mind kept returning to his last conversation that day with a woman from New York whose daughter was struggling with depression. Their conversation had transported him back to the weeks after the accident when he had fallen into a deep despair.

"My name is Laura Kilpatrick," she said, introducing herself. "My daughter has been struggling with depression these past four years, and I desperately want to help her. I've read extensively on the subject, and I've talked to many experts, but I feel like I need a new perspective, a breakthrough idea, something that reframes the conversation."

The evening air had been cooler than usual, and Daniel was mindful that he didn't want to speak about his own struggle with depression in the mountains. He had sincerely wondered whether it was because he didn't want the conversation to be about him or whether it was too painful.

Either way, he had tried to make himself fully present to Laura. And now, his mind continued to recall their conversation.

"Breakthrough idea. Reframe the conversation," Daniel had said, repeating Laura's words, as if he was talking to himself. "These ideas demonstrate that you haven't lost your curiosity around what depression is and what it isn't. That openness is essential to the type of breakthrough you are seeking.

"A psychiatrist came to visit about a year ago," Daniel continued. "He asked about new ways to approach patients experiencing depression. I suggested that he reflect on three questions: If you were treating the first patient ever to present with symptoms of depression, what would you be curious about? Is depression a disease or a symptom? How would you treat patients if medication was not available?

"I wasn't suggesting that he stop using medication. I was simply suggesting that these questions might lead to new insights.

"If there is one idea needed to reframe the conversation around depression, it may be that depression isn't a human malfunction. It's a messenger. We look at depression as an indication that something is wrong, when in fact, it may be better characterized as an indication that something is right. Depression is proof that all the highly intricate systems within you are working. It's an alarm sounding within, warning you that all is not well and that adjustments are needed.

"Or perhaps the breakthrough idea surrounds the poverty of meaning in our society. Our culture has rejected meaning and substance in favor of appearance and entertainment. The collateral damage this shift has caused in our lives is momentous. We cannot live meaningful lives by filling them with meaningless things and activities.

"And maybe the increasing depression in society is the result of the collective anger and resentment we feel toward the sheer meaninglessness that is being served up to us on a daily basis. This all-pervasive meaninglessness is eating away at our souls, and that's making people angry, whether they are aware of it or not. Ignore that anger long enough, and it will ferment and erupt into rage. This may explain all the rage we are witnessing in society."

Daniel paused for a moment. Laura was fascinated. She wished she had been recording their conversation. But as she traveled back to the city on the train that night, she reflected on some of the insights Daniel had shared:

"Depression is always trying to share a profound message about our lives and who we are becoming."

"Depression is a manifestation of unmet needs. It is always asking: What needs are not being met in your life?"

"People have been howling at the moon for decades about the adverse effects of junk food. Yes, junk food makes us physically sick, but 'junk ideas' make our minds sick and 'junk values' make our souls sick. The fundamental problem with junk food is that it doesn't meet our nutritional needs. Junk ideas don't fulfill our intellectual and psychological needs, and junk values don't meet our spiritual needs. All this junk is rotting our bodies, minds, souls, and leaves us starving."

"When we ignore what matters most in favor of what's trivial and superficial, there will always be consequences. These consequences are simply reminders of who we are, how we function best, and the changes we need to make."

"Depression is the most appropriate response to some situations in life."

"Sometimes depression is caused by a chemical imbalance in our brains, but we don't spend enough time exploring the causes behind that chemical imbalance or what changes to our lifestyle could restore the much-needed balance."

"When you get depressed, it's an indication that your whole self—heart, mind, body, and soul—is trying to get your attention and alert you to a problem."

"Perhaps the imbalance is in the way we live our lives."

As Laura's train pulled into Grand Central Station, Daniel was sitting in his living room, recalling their conversation from earlier that day. He began to examine his own life. He knew he couldn't continue doing what he was doing indefinitely, and this led him to reflect on his own unmet needs and the adjustments he needed to make to his own life.

## 41. EZRA'S GRATITUDE

When Daniel stepped out his front door the next morning, Ezra was there waiting for him. "What are you doing here?" Daniel said jovially. "This is your busiest time at the store!"

Ezra deflected Daniel's comments, and pointing to the small table beside his rocking chair, he said, "I brought you a bag of oatmeal raisin cookies, with extra cinnamon, exactly the way you like 'em."

"You are so good to me, Ezra. Thank you."

"How can I help, Daniel?"

"Ah, yes... has Sean told you about the gathering we're planning?"

"It's a wonderful idea. Everyone is so excited," Ezra replied.

"I want to do everything we can to make them feel welcome and ensure everyone has a great time. So, I was hoping you could arrange a selection of your marvelous sandwiches, cakes, cookies, and beverages. Let Sean know the cost. These are my guests, and I want to cover everything."

Ezra began laughing. "Those people are right."

"Which people?" Daniel asked, perplexed.

"The ones who say you're a lunatic, that you lost your mind in the mountains." Daniel smiled and nodded as Ezra continued. "I would never charge you, Daniel. You? You! The man who gave me the courage to chase my dream so late in life. Charge you? Never. Everything shall be as you wish, my friend."

"You are a stubborn man, Ezra Abrams. What would your Moses say about disobeying a prophet?" Daniel joked.

Ezra shot back, "What would your Jesus say about not graciously accepting gifts that are offered to you out of love and respect?"

Daniel smiled, and his smile became a laugh, and then, taking Ezra in his arms, he hugged him and whispered in his ear, "I love you, brother. Thank you for your goodness."

Ezra made his way down the old white steps and strode purposefully down the street toward the town square. He loved walking. It gave him time to think. This morning, his mind was swept away in thoughts of how much his life had changed over the past couple of years.

"Why me?" At first, Ezra was unable to let go of that question. It confounded him. But with Daniel's help, he had made peace with it now. It was a gift and a mystery, and he had learned that if you obsess over trying to understand mysteries, you miss out on enjoying them.

## 42. ANTICIPATION

Over the days that followed, news of the gathering lit up the town. The anticipation was visceral. Everywhere you went, people were talking about it. Tony, Sean, and Ezra were inundated with questions about what to expect on the night.

On the Wednesday before the gathering, Sean approached Daniel. "There's a lot of speculation about what people should expect on Sunday."

"It's their night," Daniel replied. "We can do anything they'd like. This is for them. We can mingle on the lawn, I can meet with people one at a time, we can have a conversation as a group, or we can socialize and have music and dancing."

"People have a lot of questions," Sean replied, wringing his hands nervously. "It might be good to let them raise topics and ask questions in a group setting."

"Great, then that's what we'll do," Daniel confirmed. "Spread the word so people have a few days to think about what they'd like to discuss."

## 43. SLEEPLESS NIGHT

The night before the gathering, Daniel lay awake wondering what to expect from the people of the town he had grown up in. They knew almost everything there was to know about his life, so it must have been strange for them to watch the events of the past couple of years unfold in the streets of their hometown.

New people came and went every day. Lots of them. Daniel wondered how much unspoken animosity there might be toward him for transforming their quiet little town into a community bustling with people and activity.

Many jobs had been created, businesses were thriving, and all this provided more tax dollars for their schools, roads, and hospitals. But Daniel knew there were others who cursed the changes his presence had brought to the town. They seemed unwilling or unable to acknowledge the tremendous good that was being done for so many people.

"Why doesn't he travel around visiting people instead of making them all come to him? Let the circus go from town to town and minimize the disruption to our lives," he had overheard one man grumbling.

As the sun rose, Daniel was still awake. He loved Sunday mornings. He began his morning routines before making his way down to the town square. After church, he sat in his rocking chair and visited with people until four o'clock.

At that time, Sean reminded people what he had announced earlier that day and the day before. The people gathered their things and made their way to the hotel in town. A school bus had been arranged to take the sick and the elderly.

At the hotel they were greeted with refreshments.

"How can I help?" Daniel asked Ezra.

"You can help by going inside and resting. It's going to be a big night."

*I am tired*, Daniel thought to himself, and he decided to go upstairs and take a nap before his guests arrived.

Once the crowd had dispersed, Ezra and a team of people began to set everything up. Within forty-five minutes, Daniel's front yard had come to life in a whole new way.

The lawn was covered with chairs and tables. There were teal tablecloths and white napkins. The pathway was lined with lanterns, and the banquet tables were overflowing with mouth-watering food and bottles on ice. As the sun was setting, Daniel's front yard was ablaze in a saffron glow.

## 44. A Midsummer Night

Daniel had fallen into a deep sleep. He felt groggy as he began to stir at the sound of voices outside. Getting up, he showered, dressed, and eagerly went down to greet his guests.

The townspeople began arriving just before six o'clock, and within fifteen minutes almost everyone who lived in town was in Daniel's front yard. The police chief had closed the street at both ends to ensure the residents' privacy and safety.

Daniel was mingling among the crowd, welcoming people and ensuring everyone had something to eat and drink.

"What can I get you?" Ezra asked Daniel.

"Don't worry about me, Ezra. Let's make sure everyone else has what they need."

"We have everyone taken care of, Daniel. What can I get you?" Ezra pressed.

"Umm . . . okay. Thanks. Surprise me."

"Great. I'll bring you a glass of the peach lemonade I made today. It's exactly what you need to get you through an evening of discussion," Ezra said and smiled. His excitement was contagious.

He began to walk away, but then stopped himself. Turning around, Ezra walked back to Daniel, placed a hand on his shoulder, and whispered in his ear, "This is going to be a wonderful evening. Enjoy yourself. Everything is going to be fine."

Daniel nodded appreciatively, and Ezra went to get him a drink. *Even prophets need some encouragement every now and then*, Ezra thought to himself. He knew Daniel didn't like being called a prophet, and he only ever referred to himself that way jokingly, but Ezra had also seen firsthand what God had done through him.

As seven o'clock came around, Daniel made his way to the top of the white steps that led to the front porch. He didn't have to call the crowd to attention; they hushed themselves as they saw him walking up the steps.

His guests gathered around him, forming an intimate, natural amphitheater. The children sat at the front, their innocent faces looking up expectantly. Daniel's warm and welcoming presence drew the crowd nearer. As he looked around at these men and women he had known his whole life, a series of memories flashed through his mind like fireworks. He smiled, and his whole face radiated joy.

"Welcome, my friends. Thank you for coming. As I walked up these stairs now onto Charlie's porch, I cannot help but think of him.

"What a wonderful evening!" Daniel announced with his arms outstretched, as if to embrace the whole town. "As I look around, I see faces . . . so many familiar faces. I also see memories of moments shared. Some delightfully ordinary, others extraordinary. Some fabulous, others sad and tragic. But these memories bind us together as a community.

"Charlie would be glad we are here tonight. I wish he was with us." At this, Daniel's eyes filled with tears. It didn't seem like he was going to cry, but then, a single tear escaped his left eye and ran down his cheek.

"I miss my friend," Daniel confessed tearfully. "He represented everything that is good about our town, so whatever you are drinking, please take up your glass, and let's raise a toast to a man we all knew and loved."

Lifting his glass high into the air, Daniel cheered, "To Charlie!"

"To Charlie!" the crowd replied enthusiastically.

"Thank you. I especially want to thank our friends, Sean, Tony, and Ezra for everything they have done to bring us together tonight." The crowd broke out into spontaneous applause. Those standing around the three men shook their hands, and Daniel noticed their wives holding them a little closer.

Daniel paused, allowing the moment to unfold fully. It was one of the many lessons nature had taught him in the mountains.

Then clearing his throat, he continued, "Many of you have known me since I was a boy. Tonight is for you, and my hope is that we can discuss whatever is on your hearts."

The people applauded again, and Sean made his way halfway up the stairs to Charlie's porch. "I know many of you have topics you'd like to raise with Daniel. I suggest we present them one at a time. Who would like to begin?"

## 45. THE MEANING OF LIFE

Dimitri was the oldest person in town. Everyone called him the old Greek. He called himself the old Greek. He was sitting toward the back of the group tonight, surveying the scene, and now, getting to his feet, he began to speak.

"My dear friend, thank you for inviting us to your home. You honor us with your hospitality and generosity. I came from Greece to this country as a child over eighty years ago, and this town welcomed me and nurtured me, in the same way it has nurtured my family for generations since. I have watched my children and their children grow up here. And now I'm blessed to watch my great-grandchildren enjoying this place we call home.

"It is widely believed that you are a prophet. I don't know if that is so. I have thought much about it, and I have come to the conclusion that whether you are or are not, it doesn't matter to me. What I know is that you've been given great wisdom, God has healed and comforted many people through you, and you conduct yourself with humility and discipline.

"It is written: 'By their fruits you shall know them.'

"As you can see, I'm not a young man anymore, and perhaps I'm starting to ramble, so let me come to it.

*"Speak to us about* THE MEANING OF LIFE."

"Thank you, my old friend," Daniel said in reply. "You've been a friend to my family and a friend to this town. Your words honor me, but your presence honors us all. This is a great topic to begin our conversation this evening, because the answer to every other question will have its roots in this foundational question: What is the meaning of life?

"Anything that is healthy tends toward the fullest expression of itself. Your essential purpose is to become the-best-version-of-yourself. This is the central task of your life.

"This purpose animates us. It literally breathes life into us. This single principle brings clarity to every aspect of our lives and helps to answer so many of our questions. What is the essential quality of friendship? A good friend encourages and challenges you to become a-better-version-of-yourself. What is the essential quality of fine food, a book that stirs your soul, and music that elevates? They contribute to your fullest expression.

"Everything makes sense in relation to your essential purpose. If your life doesn't make sense, you have lost the connection between your daily activity and your essential purpose. Some things help you become a-better-version-of-yourself, and some things don't. Embrace the things that do and reject those that don't. This is how we live this principle in each moment of each day. You don't need anyone to give you a list. Somewhere deep inside, you already know.

"Life is choices. We build our lives one choice at a time. We build our very selves with our choices. The moment of decision is the locus of influence that directs our lives.

"Let this question be your guide: Which path will help you become the-best-version-of-yourself? And remember in moments of doubt and confusion that anyone or anything that doesn't help you become a-better-version-of-yourself is too small for you.

"Modern minds are skeptical, even cynical, about the idea that our existence might have some universal meaning and purpose. Popular culture mocks the phrase *the meaning of life*. So it should come as no surprise that so many people's lives are marked by hopelessness. When we lose the connection between our daily activity and the greater meaning of life, despair may come gradually, but it is inevitable.

"I'll say it again: Your essential purpose is to become the-best-version-of-yourself. Can this single idea change your life? Yes! As the North Star guides sailors home, this concept will guide you through the many seasons of life. Place this idea at the center of your life. Make each decision with your purpose in mind. You will be amazed how quickly this one concept begins to transform you and your life.

"Life isn't about doing or having. It's about becoming. Who you become is infinitely more important than what you do or what you have."

The crowd was still and quiet now. Daniel turned toward Dimitri and the old Greek held his gaze. The two men looked deep into each other's eyes, before Dimitri nodded ever so slightly. The mutual respect was palpable, and the tone had been set for an epic evening of conversation.

## 46. THE GOD QUESTION

The people had settled in now. Dimitri's calm leadership and the soothing tones of Daniel's voice had banished any restlessness. The Rabbi was next to speak.

"Daniel, I admire your work, and you know I respect you, but I must question you on the point you have just made, as it is foundational to every other question and every other answer."

The crowd perked up, sensing tension, but there was none. There was humility in the Rabbi's voice. He wasn't speaking to be heard: he sincerely desired to understand what Daniel was saying.

"Our discussion is only beginning," the Rabbi continued, "and I don't want to scrutinize your very first response, so please accept my question in the spirit in which it is presented. It's not a spirit of challenge or criticism, but a spirit that seeks to understand more clearly what you are sharing with us."

Daniel nodded and smiled affirmingly at the Rabbi, extending his right hand. "Please go on."

"It is written: 'Love the Lord your God with all your heart, and with all your soul, and with all your strength,'" the Rabbi said. "My people have been taught since we were children that this is the purpose of life. Do you disagree?"

The pastor was standing next to the Rabbi, and Daniel noticed him nodding thoughtfully.

"Your mind is naturally drawn to the sixth chapter of Deuteronomy," Daniel began in reply. "No doubt the pastor's mind is drawn to the twenty-second chapter of Matthew, where Jesus is asked which is the greatest commandment. He replies by quoting Deuteronomy: 'Love the Lord your God with all your heart and with all your soul and with all your mind.' And he added to it, 'This is the first and greatest commandment. And the second is like it: Love your neighbor as yourself.'"

"Indeed," responded the Rabbi. "You are reading my mind, Daniel."

Daniel's voice was gentle but firm. He spoke with authority, and the power of his ideas were persuasive, but he was detached from the need to convince anyone. It was as if he were holding out a handful of fine jewels and asking, "Would you like some of these?"

"You raise an important question, Rabbi Joshua, and we thank you for it. Your question leads us to another crucial question: What is the best way to love God?

"Rabbi Zusya once reflected, 'In the coming world, they will not ask me: Zusya, why were you not more like Moses? They will ask me: Zusya, why were you not more like Zusya?' The world doesn't need another Moses or another Mother Teresa. It doesn't need another Rabbi Zusya or another Francis of Assisi. The world needs you.

"The best thing you can do for those you love, the strangers who cross your path, the whole world, and even those who will be born in the future, is to become a-better-version-of-yourself each day. You cannot do this and not grow in character and virtue. You cannot grow in character and virtue and not profoundly love God and neighbor. Is there a better way to love God than by becoming all He created you to be?

"What you say to your people, Rabbi, and what the pastor says to his people, and what I'm saying are not incongruent. But as I look around, I see Jews and Christians, Muslims, Hindus and Buddhists, atheists and agnostics. My calling is to speak to everyone in a way that allows each person to take the next step in their personal journey. My mission is to cast the broadest net possible so that as many people as possible can participate in these great truths.

"I trust that you can translate what I'm saying into your own tradition, and I trust that the pastor and others here tonight can do the same."

The Rabbi raised the palm of his hand in Daniel's direction to acknowledge him and said, "Thank you, my friend. The Spirit of God is upon you." And those standing close to the Rabbi heard him say to the pastor ever so quietly, "Truly, this man is a prophet sent by God to the people of our time."

## 47. GRATITUDE

The crowd was quiet and reflective now.

The air was warm and heavy, and another voice emerged from the crowd. It was George, the grocer. Her full name was Georgina, but she was affectionately known as George by everyone in town. She was the most stunningly beautiful woman within a hundred miles, even at sixty-two years old.

Everyone knew immediately the topic Georgina would raise with Daniel. She was legendary for the question she asked every customer, every day, in her grocery store: What are you grateful for today?

"My whole life I have observed the difference gratitude makes in a person's life," Georgina said joyfully.

*"Speak to us about GRATITUDE."*

"Everything is a gift," Daniel began. "We come into this world with nothing, and life lavishes upon us so many gifts.

"Joy is the fruit of appreciation. Appreciation is the ordinary and endless meditation on all that is good, true, and beautiful in our lives. When we recognize and enjoy the people, places, things, experiences, and opportunities that life is lavishing upon us, our hearts erupt with joy. And out of this meditation, the immense thankfulness of gratitude bursts forth.

"We have so much to be grateful for: fresh water, the human touch, sunlight, clothing, work, health, food, friendship, nature, learning, family, music, books, art, our bodies, fresh air, somewhere to call home, hot showers and cold streams, laughter, flowers, animals, teachers, doctors, nurses, dancing, beaches, leisure, sleep, the ability to think and dream, freedom, unexpected gifts, kind strangers, comfortable chairs, autumn leaves, a first kiss, endorphins, memories, inspiration, education, rocking chairs . . . and chocolate!" Daniel said with a smile, and the people chuckled.

"Every relationship deteriorates when we take each other for granted. You are in relationship with family and friends, but you are also in relationship with nature, your senses, and every opportunity life lays at your doorstep. Any fool can appreciate health when he is sick or his beloved when she is gone. The great challenge of life is to stay awake and aware. Appreciate your health when you are healthy; don't wait until you are sick. For the highly aware, eminently conscious soul, life becomes a litany of gratitude.

"It was gratitude that rescued me from my grief, depression, and self-pity in the mountains. Everything had been stripped from me. It wasn't until I began to be grateful for the smallest things that I came back to life. And it was only then that I realized how much I had taken for granted my whole life.

"When I'm ungrateful, I become irritable, restless, and discontent.

"When I'm not in the state of gratitude, the only way for me to be happy is for everything to go my way. This leaves me wrestling with the whole universe and everyone in it, trying to impose my will, to stretch the fabric of reality, which of course is a fool's errand. But when I'm grateful, nothing bothers me. It's impossible to be grateful and unhappy at the same time.

"Gratitude is a leading indicator of spiritual and emotional health. To be ungrateful is to be disconnected from reality, and denial of reality is a form of mental illness, however mild or severe.

"The wisdom of opposites is always revealing. What's the opposite of gratitude? Ingratitude? No. The opposite of gratitude is an eight-headed monster. The eight heads are: entitlement, incivility, ignorance, preoccupation with self, disrespect, moodiness, contempt, and ingratitude. Ingratitude is a toxic mindset that rots the soul.

"Gratitude, by contrast, holds great power. It banishes entitlement and gives birth to empowerment. Few things will alter your spiritual state faster than gratitude. More than an idea, gratitude is a way of life. It changes the way we feel about ourselves, life, and other people. It's a mind-altering disposition even in the midst of life's most difficult circumstances and an essential part of a balanced psychological diet.

"So, where does one begin? Begin with the people in your life. It's a magnificent thing to be appreciated. There are eight billion people on this planet, and I suspect 7.9 billion of them go to bed each night starving for one honest word of appreciation.

"Gratitude can single-handedly transform a relationship, for two grateful people will always have a better relationship than two ungrateful people.

"Gratitude is a higher form of consciousness, a way to anchor ourselves in the present moment and in eternity simultaneously. It's a way to bow down and show the appropriate reverence for life."

## 48. THE CRITIC

Daniel looked out at the people. Their faces were glowing. He had never witnessed a group of people so still and quiet, and he knew this was a rare moment to be cherished. But that peace was suddenly broken by harsh words that were maliciously cruel. And Daniel was reminded that words can be a form of violence.

Someone on the edge of the gathering started shouting, "You are a charlatan! You may have them fooled, but I see right through you. This whole thing is a circus, and I refuse to participate in such a charade."

The man was pushing his way through the crowd now toward the bottom of the steps. Then, turning his back on Daniel, he addressed the crowd: "Why are you so easily fooled? Can't you see? This man is a fraud, an impostor, a pretender. Have you forgotten what he did on Wall Street, living off the hard work of others, producing nothing himself but profiting like a king?"

It was Steve, the naysayer of the town. The skeptic, the cynic, the local critic of all things. Most communities have at least one. A self-appointed king of a nonexistent kingdom.

Several people tried to silence him, but Daniel raised a hand and said, "Let him be. Let him speak."

"I don't need your fake magnanimity," Steve sneered resentfully, turning to face off with Daniel. "You may be able to deceive all these people, but you can't fool me. How long will we let this circus carry on?" he cried, turning back to those around him.

"This man—"

"He has a name," someone interrupted loudly.

"His name is Daniel," someone else added.

"This man has taken over our town," Steve continued, ignoring them. "He has ruined our quiet, peaceful corner of the world. More and more people come to town every day seeking advice from this charlatan."

"What about all the good he has done?" someone called out.

"What good?" Steve replied. "You are being deceived. He calls himself a prophet. What a joke!"

"He has never called himself a prophet," someone interjected.

"Who appointed you to judge him and represent us?" someone else called out.

Steve shook his head at them. "Somebody has to watch out for you fools. I'm here to protect you from yourselves," he answered resentfully.

"What qualifies you for that illustrious post?" the mayor challenged.

"I have always had a very strong sense of justice," Steve announced boastfully, "and I sense that what's happening here is wrong and doing more harm than good."

Daniel remained silent.

When Steve had started speaking, the crowd's instinct was to protect Daniel. But they realized now that Daniel didn't need to be protected. He gave Steve his full attention.

As Steve continued speaking, the people's anger toward him dissipated into communal pity. They began to see him for what he was—a deeply unhappy man.

At that moment, Ezra remembered something Daniel had said to him when the crowds first started arriving: "Be gentle with everyone who comes here. Everyone you will meet here is carrying a heavy burden. We may never know their burden, but we are called to receive them graciously and help them in whatever ways we can. People will be rude. They will violate the spirit of this place. They will frustrate you and make you angry. But remember, it's often those who are the most disrespectful that most need our respect. It is often those who are most offensive that have the deepest wounds."

Ezra wondered what had happened to Steve for him to choose this path. He wondered what pain had caused such a deep wound.

Steve continued ranting for a few more minutes, and people started to lose interest, but not Daniel. He was as attentive and respectful as he had been to Dimitri, Georgina, the Rabbi, the Pastor, and all the others.

"What do you have to say for yourself?" Steve finally asked Daniel angrily.

Daniel didn't respond immediately. Impatient adrenaline was now rushing through Steve's veins, and he mocked Daniel, snarling, "What's the matter? Nothing to say, prophet?"

A moment of silence lingered heavy in the air before Daniel spoke. There was no anger in his voice. It was calm and respectful. "You are obviously very angry, Steve, but I don't think it has anything to do with me. Though I believe it's good for you to explore that anger, and if this helps, I'm happy to serve as your punching bag. But I suspect you look for new punching bags everywhere you go."

"How dare you—" Steve raged, interrupting Daniel.

Daniel raised his hand, saying, "I let you speak, hurling all sorts of insults and accusations at me, and I didn't interrupt you. I would appreciate the same courtesy."

Javier's mind drifted to something Daniel had said to him a few weeks earlier. "Many people think you are weak if you are kind and gentle. They see humility and generosity as weakness. Nothing could be further from the truth. All virtue requires tremendous inner strength to be sustained." As he stood on the porch of Charlie's old home now, Daniel's astounding strength was on full display.

"You accuse me of being a clown, and my life of being a circus," Daniel continued. "You call this a charade and me a pretender and impostor. Perhaps you think you are an impostor. Maybe you think your own life is a joke?"

Offended, Steve tried to interrupt again, but as before, Daniel raised his hand, firmed up his voice, and Steve backed off.

"If I wanted to fool people, my hometown is the last place I would have come. I came back here because I knew the people of this place would keep me grounded. I know my gifts and the dangers that come with them—pride being first among them. It's usually the thing that stands between us and a much better life. I know my humanity, my weaknesses, my brokenness. And I knew when I came home that the people of this town would protect me from the world and from myself.

"It is written: 'A prophet is not welcome in his own town.'

"This is more proof that I'm not a prophet, for I have never felt more welcome anywhere in my life, especially since I returned from the mountains.

"You say you have a strong sense of justice and declare yourself a defender of truth, and yet, you know very well that I have never called myself a prophet."

Daniel's voice was still calm, and though he was sharing difficult truths, there was no malice in his tone.

"Of everything that has happened here tonight, your performance most resembles a circus. I saw you there all night, lurking in the shadows, fidgeting restlessly, and waiting for your moment. You came here tonight to confront me. You had it all planned out in your mind. But now that you've had your moment, do you feel content and satisfied? I think not. When was the last time you felt content and satisfied?

"Steve, I have known you my whole life, and I don't think I've ever seen you happy for more than an hour. It doesn't matter what's happening in this town—you always know better, and you feel it's your duty to point out the problems. If you asked the people who know you best to describe you, I suspect they would say you are irritable, restless, and discontent.

"It is written: 'Judge a tree by its fruit.'

"What's wrong with the fruit being borne in this season of my life? Your criticisms seem to be long on personal attacks and short on specific objections. Have I advised people poorly? Do you disagree with the ideas I have shared? Are you opposed to the sick being healed?

"You are right that my life before I went into the mountains was self-centered. I agree. You have no argument from me there. But one of the biggest mistakes we can make, especially in small towns like ours, is not allowing people to change. Surely you can see that I'm trying to change and grow and become a better human being.

"I am not my past. I am not the things that have happened to me. I wasn't perfect in the past, and I'm not perfect now. But I need you to release me from my past so I can embrace a-better-version-of-myself. Why do you refuse? Perhaps you also need to release yourself from your past.

"One of the main reasons people don't change—and believe me, we all want to change—is because other people don't let them change. When someone begins to change and grow, we often feel judged and challenged and threatened. It isn't because that person is judging us, but because simply by changing, their mere presence challenges *us* to grow too.

"Every town has a thief and a whore and a screw-up and a miserly rich person. Sometimes, we don't want these people to change, because in the sickest ways, they make us feel good about ourselves. We use them as scapegoats. We cast all our darkness upon them because we don't want to confront the darkness within ourselves. And when the Sabbath comes, we go to our churches and synagogues, and we pray as it is written: 'God, I thank you that I am not like other people—thieves, evildoers, adulterers, and tax collectors.' But what about the thief, the whore, the screw-up, and the miserly rich person in each of us?

"You knew me as a boy. I was careless at times. You knew me as a young man. I was selfish at times. But now I'm living in your midst, trying to be a better man. Please let me. Liberate me from the inadequacies of my past, so that I can become the better man of my future."

Steve was boiling over now. "Enough. Enough!" he yelled. "You are smart and eloquent, but I'm not fooled. You may have everyone else duped, but not me. I know you are not who you pretend to be."

"Who am I pretending to be?" Daniel asked sincerely.

"A prophet, a healer, a visionary, a sage, a spiritual master . . ."

"Have I ever claimed to be any of those things?"

"That's not the point. It doesn't matter what you claim. You have all these other fools to do your bidding for you," Steve lashed out.

"So, everyone is a fool except you?" Daniel inquired.

Steve didn't know what to say, but he refused to stay silent. He considered that a failure, so he started rambling.

"Let's leave me out of it for a moment, Steve," Daniel said when he finished ranting. "Consider Georgina's question. What are you grateful for today?"

The question took Steve off guard and aggravated him even more. His eyes raged like a bull in the ring. "Why does that matter?" he retorted.

"It matters because, despite what you think of me, I still want what is good for you. I want you to find peace and contentment. These things are only possible if we give grateful homage to the good people, things, opportunities, and experiences in life, and to the Giver of all good things.

"My own experience has been that when I am grateful, very little bothers me. It seems that everything bothers you. So, it makes me wonder if you are grateful."

"Are you trying to embarrass me?" Steve said angrily.

"No, I'm not trying to embarrass you. Perhaps you feel that way because you were trying to embarrass me. It's natural to project your motives upon me, but they are not real."

Daniel made his way down the steps and stood before Steve. "Forget that everyone else is here for a moment," Daniel said softly so that only Steve could hear. It was an invitation to an intimate moment. "It's just you and me now. Man to man. Neighbor to neighbor." But Steve pulled away.

"Don't play mind games with me!" Steve lashed out, rejecting Daniel's invitation. "I'm not going to let you brainwash me like you've brainwashed everyone else."

Steve turned to walk away, but then rounded on Daniel one more time with rage in his eyes, and yelled, "Listen, kid . . ."

"He's not a kid," someone interrupted.

"He's a prophet," someone else added.

"The rocking chair prophet," Ezra whispered quietly to himself.

Steve had worn himself out. He turned his back on Daniel, put his head down, and walked away bitterly. He was angry. It was consuming him. But what he was so angry about, nobody knew. Most people felt relieved as he walked away, but in that moment, as everyone's eyes were fixed on Steve, Ezra looked up toward Daniel.

Perhaps it was out of concern, or perhaps it was a reflex. He wasn't sure. But what he saw in Daniel's face moved him more than anything he had experienced that evening. There was a profound sadness in Daniel's eyes as the critic, the naysayer, the skeptic, the cynic walked away. Ezra had an overwhelming desire to know what was going through Daniel's mind in that moment.

He would ask him, but not now. He tucked the memory away for another time and place.

## 49. A HEAVY MOOD

The mood of the evening had changed. A shadow had been cast over the gathering and a heavy feeling came over the crowd. Tony looked at Sean, and Sean looked at Ezra, who shrugged. They knew the festivities needed to be rescued, but they didn't know how to do it.

Dimitri was an observant man and an unrivaled host. It was not his party, but he noticed the three men were perplexed and he acted instinctively. "Who needs another drink?" he roared jovially from the back of the lawn. People laughed and raised their glasses, and the mood of the evening had been restored.

Ezra looked at Dimitri, waited until he caught his eye, and nodded to him gently as he tapped his heart twice with his right hand. Dimitri removed his trilby hat, bowed gently in Ezra's direction, and smiled. Like an elder statesman, he had read the situation perfectly and effortlessly rescued the evening with the light touch of humor.

Before too long, Daniel began to speak again. "There is much we could discuss about Steve's comments, and I'm happy to if you wish. But it's important to me that we are all on the same page about one thing."

He paused and thirstily gulped down some of his lemonade. This gave everyone a chance to settle back into their seats. It was clear that what Daniel was about to say was important.

"Tonight you are my guests," he continued, "but I consider myself very much your guest here in this town. If I was simply living here and working a regular job, and coming and going like anyone else, I wouldn't feel that way. But all the visitors and the disruption to the way things have been around here for a hundred years makes it different.

"So tonight, while we are all here together, I want to make a pledge to you as a community. I declare to each of you that I will leave here tomorrow morning if you wish. It matters to me that you know that the destiny of this town is still in your hands, not mine, and not the thousands of visitors who come here each month. If at any time in the future you come to me, united in your conviction that it would be best if I were to move on to another place, I won't argue or object. Within three days, I'll be gone. This is my pledge to you."

The people were grateful he had made this offer, but they hoped they would never have to call him on his pledge. Still, Daniel knew that if he stayed there long enough, at some point, that day would come.

## 50. HEALTH

Daniel's childhood friend Javier, the doctor, was the next person to speak.

"I have dedicated my life to the health of the people in this town. I deliver their babies, tend to their coughs and colds, set their broken bones, and try to comfort them in the final hours of their lives," he explained for context.

*"Speak to us about* HEALTH."

Daniel smiled warmly at his childhood friend. "Would you trade a lung for fifty dollars? Would you sell a week of good health for a thousand dollars? When placed in such brazen terms, we dismiss these proposals as ridiculous. But we barter, sell, gamble, and trade away our health in dozens of ways every day. Each day we barter with life. Some of these dealings are good and necessary. We trade our energy for a hard day's work. We exchange some time to play with our children in the park. But we make bad trades too. How unhealthy are you willing to become in order to get that next promotion?

"Health is the foundation of life. All our hopes and dreams depend upon it. Young people dream of traveling to distant lands. Parents dream of watching their children's lives unfold and playing with their grandchildren. Illness robs us of more than energy and movement; it absconds with our hopes and dreams.

"Whatever you fix your mind on will increase in your life. Set your mind on thoughts of health. Health is a mighty river pulsing through your being. Imagine this river of life flowing through your veins. Actions are not leaders; they are followers. What do they follow? Thought is a leader, and our actions follow where our thoughts lead.

"Treasure your health. Guard it like the finest treasure. We are sensitive to the ways other people wrong us, but desensitized to the ways we wrong ourselves.

"We experience life through our bodies. Our bodies are excellent servants but terrible masters. Allowing your body to rule and direct your life is a sure path to self-destruction. If we become slaves to our bodies, they begin to lie to us. This is why the wise deny their bodies in small ways each day.

"Why do we appreciate health most when we are sick? The wisdom of opposites speaks loud and clear to us through illness. Illness is a great sage. It enlightens us to what matters most and awakens our true priorities. Sleepwalking through life, we only appreciate our health when we are sick. But the wise live on a higher realm of consciousness, and they wake each morning grateful for the health that makes everything else possible.

"Lifestyle—a healthy lifestyle—is the ultimate medicine. There is a direct correlation between most people's health and their lifestyle. Medication is most efficacious when combined with a remedied lifestyle.

"When illness visits you, examine your lifestyle. A healthy lifestyle is the only lasting remedy for disease. Long before we get sick, long before we need medication or surgery, our body whispers to us, *I need this . . . I yearn for that . . .Take care of me a little better, and I will serve you well for a long time.*

"What is the secret to vibrant physical health? There is no secret. Laugh a little each day, sleep deep and long, hydrate plentifully, eat to fuel your body—not out of boredom or for entertainment—and take a long walk in a quiet place each day."

## 51. THE GOOD LIFE

A comfortable rhythm was emerging. Someone would raise a topic, Daniel would respond, and the people would reflect.

Mario, the proprietor of a small Italian restaurant in town, spoke next.

"My grandparents came from the old country decades ago. They brought with them their dreams and memories, their music and language, their cooking and history. In Italian, there is a phrase, *la dolce vita*, which means *the good life*. It seems everyone is seeking some version of it.

*"Speak to us about* THE GOOD LIFE."

"Each person idealizes *la dolce vita* in their own way," Daniel responded. "What do you imagine when you think of the good life? Pleasure, possessions, prosperity, food, wine, travel, independence, exquisite clothing, carefree living, dancing, success, lovemaking, reckless abandon, financial freedom, tranquility, escape?

"Many of these things can play a role, but they are not the essence of the good life. We know this to be true because even with an abundance of all these things, you can still live a tragically empty life. And it is the essence that we seek in all things.

"We all have a vision of the good life, and at the same time, we pretend to be baffled by it.

"What is the secret to the good life? The answer is gloriously simple: goodness itself. You cannot have an ocean without water, and you cannot authentically experience the good life without goodness. The secret to the good life is goodness itself. It's the essential ingredient. It is the essence.

"So, fill your life with goodness. This is the path that leads to the good life. Fill your life with wisdom, friendship, generosity, patience, kindness, courage, justice, service, honesty, humility, and love. Your heart glows and your soul shines when you embrace, celebrate, and perpetuate goodness.

"Goodness is what you desire, and you are most beautifully and wonderfully yourself in goodness."

## 52. PARENTS AND CHILDREN

Fiona was new to town. In her middle thirties, she was the mother of three young children. Daniel had seen them riding their bikes up and down the street. As she began to speak, he thought of his own mother.

*"Speak to us about* PARENTS AND CHILDREN."

"We are all children of life. Our sons and daughters are this generation reaching out for the next, and their loins will ache for another generation yet to come.

"Everyone is someone's son or daughter. When we stop seeing people in this light, our worldview becomes distorted, and a tragic dehumanization begins.

"It is written: 'Begin with the end in mind.'

"If ever something was worthy of intentionality, it's parenting. There is a dream you hold in your heart for your children. You yearn for your sons and daughters to become the-best-version-of-themselves. This is the universal parental dream because it is the Divine parental dream.

"Parents often come to visit me here on the porch and ask how to be better parents. This is what I say to them: Walk into town and sit on one of the benches in the square. Write a brief vision of the person you hope your child will be at twenty-one, thirty-five, and fifty. Meditate on that vision for one minute each day, and parent toward that vision. Make decisions based on that vision and advise your children with that vision in mind. Love your child toward that vision."

## 53. MONEY AND THINGS

Sameer and his wife, Aisha, were traders. They imported goods from the Far East and exported local offerings on the ships as they returned to foreign lands. Aisha was next to address Daniel.

*"Speak to us about* MONEY AND THINGS."

"In the mountains, I had so little, and yet I had everything I needed. A profound providence was at work.

"The world is full of glorious things to be enjoyed. Take pleasure in them, allow them to delight you, engage them for your enjoyment and the merriment of others. But guard your heart from becoming attached to the things of this world. They will hold you down and prevent your soul from soaring.

"People were made to be loved, and things were made to be used. But if we allow our hearts to become engulfed with the love of things, sooner or later we will fall into using people to protect the things we love.

"Money can divide a person against himself. It can separate a person from her destiny.

"The secret to *right relationship* with money and things is knowing what they can and cannot accomplish. Money cannot buy the most important things: health, love, respect, character, wisdom, self-esteem, friendship, inner peace, meaning and purpose, faith, loyalty, or happiness. And money cannot buy back a squandered opportunity.

"Money is neutral. It is neither good nor bad. How we use money gives it a positive or negative charge. We have all seen money deployed in ways that are generous, thoughtful, and uplifting. But we have also seen money misused in ways that are pointless, absurd, wasteful, repulsive, and obscene.

"It doesn't matter how much money we have or don't have; the ubiquitous influence of money should make us vigilant.

"It is written: 'The thing about money is that it makes you do things you don't want to do.'

"We need so little. When we multiply our needs and desires, we diminish our happiness. Let your needs and desires be few and simple. Know how little you need to live and be happy.

"It is written: 'He who needs least has most.'

"Still, money is woven into our everyday lives, so it's wise to observe the seven unchanging laws of money: Save a portion of all that you earn. Control your expenses. Invest wisely to multiply your savings. Guard against loss. Increase your ability to earn. Ensure a future income. Be generous at every step along the way.

"May you always have enough money to attend to your needs, to be generous with others, and to follow your dreams."

## 54. SPIRITUALITY

Samuel Miller spoke now. He was an Amish farmer. His land was on the outskirts of town, adjacent to where Daniel's wife and daughters had died years ago.

Everybody loved Samuel. He was a gentle soul, a wise and generous man, always looking for opportunities to help others. You never had to ask him for anything because before you could ask, he had seen the need and offered his assistance.

"Good evening, Daniel," Samuel said cordially.

"Good evening, Mr. Miller. I am so pleased you joined us tonight. You honor us with your presence."

"Thank you. I do not wish to cause you any pain, but I think it should be said that your wife and daughters would be incredibly proud of you tonight. I hope you know that."

Daniel nodded toward Samuel and said, "Thank you, Mr. Miller," his eyes filling with tears.

"All my life I have searched for the face of God in all things," Samuel continued. "I have sought His will and yearned to know His ways.

**"Speak to us about SPIRITUALITY."**

Daniel recollected himself.

"It is written: 'The greatest threat to your happiness and wholeness is your unrecognized spiritual needs.'

"Spirituality is essential for human beings to flourish. It's as essential as air to breathe, water to drink, and the human touch. People sit here on these rocking chairs and say, 'I'm not a spiritual person,' but truly I say to you, there is no such thing.

"It is written: 'We are not human beings having a spiritual experience. We are spiritual beings having a human experience.'

"Your soul is your essence. Your most beautiful self is spiritual. Your most creative self is spiritual. Your unfathomable ability to love is spiritual. Don't abandon your essence. Alienation from God is alienation from self.

"Spirituality solves one of the fundamental human dilemmas, though it is often overlooked: It restores us to right relationship with self. The fruit of this great restoration is dynamic collaboration with God, right relationship with other people, harmony with creation, and the glorious wholeness that we spend our lives seeking.

"It is written: 'Pray constantly.'

"But we cannot simply retreat into our synagogues and churches to pray all day—there are things to be done and life to be lived.

"Yet life is a prayer—all of life. Transforming every activity into prayer is the secret to experiencing life in every breath, the secret to being fully alive. Playing catch with your son is prayer. Preparing a meal is prayer. Bathing is prayer. Work is prayer. Washing the dishes is prayer. Changing a baby's diaper is prayer. Walking is prayer. Shopping is prayer. Making love is prayer. Reading to your child is prayer.

"The primary mandate of the spiritual life is to transform everything into prayer.

"Spirituality may seem theoretical, but in truth, nothing is more practical. Consider whatever problem you are grappling with in your life. How many ways have you tried to solve that problem? Perhaps you think you have tried everything. Maybe you feel hopeless, have quit trying, have decided to live with the problem. But have you ever asked God to help? Not in a cursory way, but begged God with your whole being? And do you have a better chance of solving that problem with or without God's help?

"It is written: 'No problem can be solved from the same level of consciousness that created it.'

"Spirituality elevates our consciousness. It allows us to see life's problems and opportunities from a completely different perspective.

"Prayer, meditation, and other spiritual practices raise our consciousness. They elevate every experience to its highest state. A glass of water tastes different to someone with finely tuned spiritual awareness. The ordinary events of everyday life, like reading a book, listening to the wind in the trees, walking along a beach, or having a conversation with a friend, can all be profoundly spiritual experiences. When we are living on this plane of heightened consciousness, making love can be as transcendent as going to church on Sunday.

"It is time to stop seeking worldly solutions to spiritual problems. When was the last time you felt amazing? The moment you decide to embrace spirituality like never before, you will be closer than ever to being fully alive. Spirituality enables you to share your most consummate self with the world."

## 55. GENEROSITY

Henry was the conductor on the train to New York. Traveling back and forth to the city five days a week as people made their way to work and home again, he had received a comprehensive education in the intricacies of human nature. Henry was the next person to speak.

"Life is full of giving and receiving. My experience has divided people into two groups: those who understand the power of giving and those who don't; those who see abundance and those who see scarcity; those who see ways for everyone to win and those who see every situation as a zero-sum scenario."

*"Speak to us about GENEROSITY."*

Daniel answered, "People often express a desire to live more meaningful lives. I will tell you what I have told them: If you want to unleash an endless stream of meaning and fulfillment in your life, wake each morning eager to be more generous than you were yesterday. Don't compare your generosity to that of others. Comparison is the great limiter of human discovery.

"It is written: 'There is nothing noble in being superior to your fellow man; true nobility is being superior to your former self.'

"If you wish to discover who you are, explore the horizons of your generosity.

"Adopt the generosity habit. Give something away every day. It doesn't need to be money or material possessions. You don't need money or things to live a life of staggering generosity. There are a thousand ways to be generous. Generosity is wildly creative. It's always looking for new and interesting ways to manifest. Listen to the spirit of generosity within you. Allow it to inspire you.

"Express your appreciation. Visit someone who is lonely. Plant a tree. Support small businesses. Teach. Mentor. Coach. Make someone's day. Assist a colleague who is under pressure to finish a project. Compliment a stranger. Be a generous lover. Encourage people. Help someone who is in a hurry. Volunteer. Listen.

"Every act of generosity ennobles another human being. Generosity proclaims loud and clear: 'I see you. I hear you. You are worthy. I am with you. I care.' Generosity, by its very nature, rehumanizes.

"Generosity is creative, beautiful, life-giving, astonishing, magnanimous, visionary, encouraging, compassionate, elevating, spiritual, innovative, brilliant, proactive, courageous, and hopeful.

"Generosity holds the power to rehumanize the world. Generosity cures sick and injured cultures.

"Astound people with your generosity. Use your one short life to do the most good for the most people. Unleash the power and nobility of generosity in your life. Generosity is one of the few things in this world that still has the power to intrigue people."

## 56. WORK

Olivia was next to speak. She managed the manufacturing plant on the outskirts of town. Her role kept her busy directing the daily operations of the enterprise, but she also spent a lot of time adjudicating disputes between the workers and management.

*"Speak to us about* **WORK***."*

"Your work casts a bright light or a deep shadow on the rest of your life," Daniel told the crowd. "Like a prism, it disperses joy and satisfaction or misery and dissatisfaction to every other aspect of life.

"Work can take many forms. It could be the professional work of a career, the work of raising a family and tending to a home, the work of nurturing a talent for leisure, or the work of volunteering to improve the lives of those in need.

"Work is essential to the human experience. There is a hunger in you that can only be satisfied by work. This is a hunger the idle don't understand. They try to feed it with everything except the one thing that will satisfy it. Still, the idle have many admirers, and many more fantasize of being idle. But idleness is a curse, and most people are oblivious to the emptiness brought about by not having anything to do.

"It is written: 'Work will cure just about anything.'

"I believe that. I have experienced it. Working hard, spending ourselves worthily, and being tired—honestly tired—is good for the heart, mind, body, and soul.

"We have stumbled once more upon a gap in the human experience. We spend more time working than anything else in life, and yet we know so little about the meaning and value of work. And for all our talk of progress, one of the great tragedies of our age is how few people are well-matched with work that suits their talents and personality.

"Too many people spend their days toiling away at work that is ill-suited to their unique abilities. Why are we not taught to find something we can joyfully dedicate our lives to, while at the same time providing for our temporal needs? We have a collective responsibility to save future generations from this fate.

"To understand the role of work, begin with purpose. Some say we work to earn money and provide the necessities of life. This makes work merely a means to an end. If we accept this view, we enslave ourselves to the idea that life must be put on hold to work, and only when our work is done can we return to life. When you consider how much of our lives we spend working, this is a rather depressing view. But it is commonly held. Why? Because we have failed to understand that work is an important ingredient of a deeply fulfilling life. Work has value unto itself.

"The true meaning and value of work is revealed when we consider work as an end in itself. The money we earn from work, while necessary, is a secondary outcome. The primary value work provides is in your development as a human being. Every hour you work to the best of your ability, paying attention to the details of your work, you become a-better-version-of-yourself. Work nurtures character by providing opportunities to grow in virtue. Work increases patience, concentration, perseverance, diligence, determination, discipline, and commitment.

"Few things bring more joy in this life than discovering work you love, work you can throw yourself into with reckless abandon. This is one of the great luxuries of life.

"It is written: 'Your vocation in life is where your greatest joy meets the world's greatest need.'

"Pursue that joy and meet that need. How will you know when you have found it? It is marked by the glorious sensation of timelessness."

## 57. LEARNING

Virginia was the librarian. For forty years, she served the children in town, capturing their imaginations with the greatest stories of every age. The wisdom of these stories sank their roots deep into the children's lives. She addressed Daniel now.

"I have observed that people are reading less and less," she lamented. "I believe there is a vast difference between the performance of a child who learns to love reading and one who doesn't. But more and more, it seems our young people are being consumed by technology and other content that doesn't unlock their imagination, encourage creativity, or unleash their potential.

*"Speak to us about* LEARNING.*"*

"We find ourselves at a familiar crossroads in the area of education," Daniel began. "It's a crossroad humanity has approached time and again throughout history. Will we commit to teaching our children how to think or make the timeworn mistake of teaching them what to think?

"When I was about seven years old, I overheard my mother having a conversation with my teacher one day after school. 'I'm concerned Daniel is behind the rest of the class; we need to push him to catch up,' the teacher told my mother. I have never forgotten my mother's response: 'People don't learn at the same pace,' she said. 'It doesn't matter if he's first in the class or last. What matters is that his father and I partner with you to enflame his love of learning. If he falls in love with learning, he will become a lifelong learner and live a rich and full life. This is much more important than his grades in school.'

"Years later, I realized I didn't overhear that conversation by chance. My mother wanted my teacher to be clear about my parents' priorities around education, but she also wanted me to be clear.

"This is the question for parents, teachers, and society: What goal are we trying to accomplish with education? The word *education* comes from the Latin word *educare*, which means 'to draw out.' Modern education seems more interested in imposing specific and standardized knowledge, skills, and ideas upon our young people so they can become obedient consumers and cogs in the global economic wheel. But each child has a unique blend of talent and personality that is perfectly suited to make a unique contribution. Imagine if we could help each young person discover this world of possibilities within them!

"How would our education system change if love of learning was the focus? Radically. And that shows us how lost we are. Do we have the courage and patience to help children discover their inherent love of learning? The future of education depends on it."

## 58. NATURE

Stanley was a quiet man. He was always pleasant but kept mostly to himself. To everyone's surprise, he was the next to speak.

"You lived in the mountains for years, Daniel. I have heard people talking about your experiences, but I'm curious to understand what you learned about nature in the mountains.

"*Speak to us about* NATURE."

Daniel caught himself drifting off into reminiscence. "For years, before I went into the mountains, I would encounter nature and she would whisper, 'Your life is out of balance. You have lost your rhythm.' I would smile politely and move on, as we do when we encounter any truth we are not ready to live.

"It is written: 'Look deep, deep into nature, and then you will understand everything better.'

"When I first went into the mountains, I was grief-stricken, deeply traumatized. I was desperately trying to understand what had happened and why. I had turned in on myself trying to comprehend the enigma of suffering and random tragedy.

"Sitting here on the porch visiting with people has made me realize that we have all been traumatized in one way or another, though many people don't realize it.

"Nature is a healer. I didn't realize it at first because I was too caught up in my pain, but up in the mountains, being immersed in nature was soothing and healing. It was weeks, maybe months before I became aware that the rhythms and routines of nature were healing me. The simplicity of nature saved me from the complexity of life.

"Nature drew me out of myself. My life before the accident was at times small and self-absorbed. One night, I sat by the lake gazing up at the stars, and I started to wonder, 'When was the last time you gazed at the stars?' I couldn't remember. It had been that long.

"Our lives have become so small and self-referential that it doesn't even occur to us to look up at the night sky in awe and wonder.

"Nature teaches us how to live. She knows more about life than anyone you will ever meet. She has been observing life for millions of years.

"We tell ourselves that we are too busy, that we don't have time for her. But the more we disconnect from nature, the more impatient and unhappy we become.

"It is written: 'Adopt the pace of nature. Her secret is patience.'

"Nature rejoices in endless routine. These routines are not monotonous or boring; they are nurturing and sustaining. I saw more sunrises in those first few months in the mountains than I had seen in my entire life. The simplest routines became life-giving.

"Nature seeks to bring order to our lives with rhythm. The sun rises and sets to a rhythm. The tides rise and fall to a rhythm. The seasons come and go to a rhythm. Your heart pumps blood through your body to a rhythm. Everything in creation has rhythm. The more I became connected to the rhythm of life, the more I realized how disordered my life had been before I went into the mountains.

"When we abandon the rhythm, the result is chaos, confusion, destruction, and disorder. The further we stray from the natural rhythm of life, the more anxious and restless we become. This disease creates disease.

"The happiest and healthiest people bind their daily activity to the rhythm of life. We cannot all go off into the mountains. I know that. But I also know that we are not all called to that. We are, however, all called to unite ourselves with nature. If we spend a couple of days immersed in nature, or even a couple of hours, she will reveal how out of balance our lives have become. And she will ask us this question: Do you have the courage to step out of the madness?"

## 59. THANK YOU

The moon was high in the cloudless sky. It had been an amazing evening, and now Daniel sensed it was time to bring the conversation to a close.

"I want to thank you all for coming this evening," he announced. "This has been a deeply touching experience. Many of you have thanked me. Thank Ezra, Sean, Tony, and all those among you who have worked tirelessly to make this evening so memorable. I also extend my heartfelt gratitude to them."

Applause broke out, and Daniel paused to let the people express their appreciation.

"Finally, as a way of thanking you all for being so gracious to me since I returned from the mountains, I have a gift for you. As we envisioned this time together tonight, I wondered what the perfect way to end the evening would be.

"In doing so, I was reminded, as I often am, of my wife, Jessica. Whenever we were invited to events in the city, her first question was always, 'Will there be dancing?' Jessica loved to dance. If there wasn't dancing at the event, she made me promise that I would dance with her when we got home. And many of my fondest memories are of dancing with her in the finest ballrooms in New York City, on the sidewalk waiting for the valet, in the driveway under the stars when we got home, in the kitchen, in the living room . . ."

Daniel's voice trailed off. He was lost in a memory. When he realized what had happened, he cleared his throat and continued. "So, tonight, before you leave, I invite you to dance. I asked a band from the city to join us, and they have agreed to play until we are done dancing. So, dance with the one you love, dance with your friends and family, and if you are too old to dance, sway to the music and remember the times and places where you danced when you were younger.

"I'm so glad we were able to come together tonight. Thank you."

The townspeople stood and applauded. And as Daniel made his way down the steps from the porch, the music began to play, and he shook hands and hugged his neighbors.

## 60. BLISSFUL EXUBERANCE

The mood of the evening changed once more. The people were exuberant. Men, women, and children of all ages flooded the area that had naturally cleared to form a makeshift dance floor.

Ezra looked around, and his heart sang. Everywhere he looked, his friends and neighbors were engaged in animated conversation, dancing with each other, eating, drinking, and having the time of their lives.

It had been a rare and inspiring evening. Ezra couldn't remember the last time the town had come together and had this much fun. In fact, he had lived here for over fifty years, and he couldn't remember the town ever having come together like this before. *People will remember this night for the rest of their lives*, he thought to himself.

It was one of those moments in life that you want to hold on to, so you try to extend it, but even as you do, you feel it slipping away.

The band played a fast set and then a slow set, picked up the tempo for a moderate set, and rounded out the evening with another slow set. The sounds of celebration rose into the night sky. The people didn't want it to end. They didn't want to go home. So they danced a little more, ate a little more, drank a little more, and laughed a little more.

An older couple drifted away from the crowd, and a younger couple with sleepy children made their way home. Then one by one, people began to say good night.

Daniel was speaking to Dimitri and the Rabbi as the party began to break up. When he turned around, he saw a young couple dancing slow, cheek to cheek, in the middle of the road, and Ezra and Leah holding each other close as they danced at the bottom of the porch steps.

It was a clear night, and the stars were brighter than usual. Daniel felt a profound happiness watching these couples dance. But at the edge of that happiness was a sharp stab of grief. He missed his wife. He missed his girls. He longed for one more dance with them.

# 61. A PROUD FATHER

When everyone had gone home and Daniel finally came inside, he found his father sitting at the kitchen table. Daniel was exhausted but so happy to see him.

"Coffee?" his father asked, getting up to brew a fresh pot.

"Sure. When did you get here, Dad?"

"About ten minutes before you started speaking. I made myself some tea and a slice of that apple-cinnamon cake and sat here on the couch. I could hear everything. You were amazing, son."

"Why didn't you come outside and join us?" Daniel asked.

"I sat in the living room and cracked the window. Had the best seat in the house."

"You should have come outside. People would've loved to have seen you."

"It wasn't my place tonight. This was for the people of the town."

"But this was your hometown for more than thirty years."

"True, but still I felt it better to stay behind the scenes tonight. I wanted to hear you speak, and I didn't want to be a distraction."

"Did you come because you were worried about me, Dad?"

"Sure. That was part of it," he said with an uncomfortable smile. "And I knew your mother would be more at ease if I was here and could let her know that all was well," Daniel's father explained.

The two men sat quietly sipping their coffee, and then his father asked, "What was your favorite part of the evening?"

Daniel thought for a while.

"Three things. I loved that it brought everyone together. I know there is a lot of history in this town, disputes that have taken place over the years between individuals and families, but tonight they were able to put all that behind them. And then, the music and dancing were enchanting. It was like the whole street was overflowing with joy."

"You always did love to dance," his father said, looking at Daniel expectantly. Daniel knew what his father was thinking. They had both noticed the way some of the women looked at him, danced with him, hovered around him. But Daniel didn't respond. He just smiled, knowingly.

"What was the third thing?" his father asked.

"Throughout the evening," Daniel explained, "I had this sense that Charlie would've loved tonight." Daniel's father smiled and nodded.

Father and son sat talking for another hour or so before his father said, "I should go."

"Why don't you stay here tonight?" Daniel suggested.

"I'll be fine," his father replied.

"It's not a short drive, Dad, and it's already three o'clock. It will be five by the time you get home."

His father knew what his son wasn't saying. Daniel was thinking about the possibility of another accident. No matter how much he had evolved spiritually, the trauma of that single event years ago would never be far from him.

"You're right, son," his father conceded. "Thank you. I will stay."

Daniel got his father settled in the guest room and said good night.

"Good night, son," his father replied. And then, hugging Daniel tight, he whispered in his ear, "You're a fine man, and I am enormously proud of you. It is an honor to be your father."

"Thank you, Dad. I love you."

"Love you too, my boy."

## 62. THE MORNING AFTER

Daniel didn't sleep. He was on a natural high. He began to compare it to the ecstasy he sometimes experienced during meditation, but as he did, he realized this was a different kind of elation. He lay there on his bed, immersed in a sea of thanksgiving. It had been an exhilarating evening.

At five-thirty, he got up and quietly made his way downstairs in his pajamas. The old stairs creaked, and Daniel hoped he wouldn't wake his father.

Ezra had already stopped by. There was a batch of warm apple-cinnamon muffins on the kitchen table and fresh coffee had been brewed.

*Ezra mustn't have slept either*, Daniel mused to himself. His heart was bursting with gratitude, and he gave thanks for the love and support of so many good people throughout his life.

Daniel was almost finished with his early-morning routines when Sean came through the back door. "What a night!" the Irishman boomed.

"Yes, it was something else! Thanks again for all you did to help make it happen," Daniel said.

"I know people say this all the time, but it has never been truer. It was absolutely my pleasure, Daniel," Sean gushed.

Tony came through the door a few minutes later with his larger-than-life personality. He had Javier with him. "Look who I found," he exclaimed.

"Looks like Ezra was here early," Javier said, rubbing his hands together and eyeing the muffins.

"Yes, very early," Daniel confirmed.

"He didn't sleep," Sean said. "Neither did I. I came straight from his shop now. He told me he's been up baking all night. I have never seen him so happy."

Daniel smiled. He could see Ezra in his mind's eye, singing and dancing around the kitchen at the back of the store. He knew him so well—his mannerisms, his facial expressions, the way he gestured with his hands when he was excited to share something, the way his eyes lit up a split-second before he smiled. Daniel knew Ezra's joy, and he delighted in his friend's newfound happiness.

"He dropped off my favorite apple-cinnamon muffins. Would you like one?" Daniel asked the others. They eagerly dug in.

It was still early. The four men sat around the table, reminiscing about the night before, and Daniel enjoyed listening to them trade stories. He felt blessed to be surrounded by such fine people.

## 63. YOUR DREAMS KNOW THE WAY

It was an idyllic morning. The sun was rising toward the mountains, and a slight breeze was blowing from the east. A little before eight o'clock, Daniel made his way out onto the porch and sat in his rocking chair. His father was still asleep, and Daniel was glad.

The first person he met with that day was a woman from New Mexico who had been waiting to see Daniel for three days and was glad to have spent last night in the hotel.

"Good morning," Daniel said, smiling. "What brought you here today?"

Her name was Samantha. She was fifty-two years old, and Daniel noticed that she looked excessively tired. She had the worn-down look of someone who had been disappointed by life too many times.

Samantha and Daniel conversed for a while about her life and the questions she was wrestling with in her heart. She shared the highlights and lowlights of her story, and then an enduring silence fell between them. The only noises were the creaking of the chairs and the chirping of the birds in the trees along the street.

Samantha had lived a difficult life, and Daniel's heart was filled with empathy for her. She had made some poor choices, been misled and used, and like so many others, now found herself alone trying to make sense of her life.

"You are not what has happened to you," Daniel said gently, breaking the silence.

"I know," she agreed, unconvincingly, and sighed heavily.

"I'm not sure you do," Daniel continued. "You may know it here," he said, tapping his temple with his index finger. "But do you know it here?" tapping his heart. "And here?" pointing to his gut. "It's one thing to acknowledge it intellectually but believing it in your heart and in your gut is very different."

She sat looking at him.

"Can you say it?" Daniel prompted.

Samantha sighed. "I'm not what has happened to me," she mumbled. It was barely audible.

"I can hear in your voice that you don't believe it yet," he said. "And that's okay. Take a couple of minutes. Close your eyes and reflect on it. When you are ready, open your eyes, look me in the eye, and say it with all the conviction you can muster."

A few minutes later, she did. The change was palpable.

"Good, good," Daniel said, encouraging and affirming her. "It will take time to own that conviction, but that's how we make peace with the past."

"And then what?" Samantha pondered.

"Ah . . . then we look to the future to empower the present," he replied with a boyish grin.

"What do you mean?" she asked, perplexed.

He replied with a question of his own. "What are you looking forward to in the future?"

"I can't remember the last time I thought about the future," Samantha explained. "It's been taking all my energy trying to survive the present and get over the past."

"It is written: 'When you cry, dry your eyes, because better days are sure to come. And when you dream, dream big, as big as the ocean blue.'

"Maybe it's time to dream again," Daniel suggested. "Our dreams animate us. They breathe new life into us. They fill us with energy and enthusiasm."

Samantha looked bewildered. "I'm not even sure I know what it means to dream anymore," she confessed.

"When do you think you stopped dreaming?" Daniel asked.

Samantha thought for a bit, then as she started to speak, she paused and thought a little more before saying, "I really don't know."

"It is written: 'Where there is no vision, the people will perish.'

"Our ability to dream is an astounding gift," Daniel offered. "It's the third of the great universal gifts the Creator has endowed us with. The first is life itself, the second is free will, and the third is the ability to dream.

"To dream is the ability to look into the future, imagine something better, and then return to the present moment and take action to bring about that richly imagined future.

"Dreaming unlocks our unrealized potential. Everything that is dormant within you gets released in that moment, and you experience your pure potential. Sometimes the dream state only lasts for the briefest moment, but that is all it takes for you to see what is possible."

"I feel so lost and confused," Samantha said, deflating.

"That's okay. There was a time and a reason for that, but now that season is over. Your dreams are your dreams for a reason," Daniel said in a voice that was softer and even more comforting than usual. "Follow your dreams; they know the way."

## 64. EXHAUSTION

The day stretched on. Though he was tired, Daniel became absorbed in the narratives of his visitors' lives and lost track of time. Each person had a question, a burden, or a profound need to be seen and heard.

Before lunch, his father stepped out the front door to say goodbye. "I'm heading home, son."

"I'm glad you slept, old man," Daniel said jovially, standing to hug his father. "I called Mom this morning. Told her we would let her know when you were on your way home."

Daniel met with people all afternoon and into the evening. At six o'clock, Sean suggested that he stop for the day.

"Let's press on, Murph. Some of these people have been waiting for days."

Sean went back down the stairs and sent the next person in line up to visit with Daniel, but he was worried about his friend.

A couple of hours later, the daylight was receding, and Daniel decided to call it a day.

He was absolutely exhausted as he walked back into the house. For thirteen hours, he had been sitting in the rocking chair listening to people's hopes and heartaches. Walking up the stairs to his bedroom, Daniel couldn't remember the last time he'd been this tired, but he was also deeply satisfied. He didn't eat or shower. He didn't even change into his pajamas. He slid off his shoes, lay down, and fell into a deep and restorative sleep.

## 65. EVERYONE'S CURIOUS

A young man stopped Daniel in the street a few days later to ask him a question. It was the question so many people had wanted to ask at different times and in different ways. It was a question some felt Daniel had been avoiding ever since he came down from the mountains.

"What happened in the mountains?" the young man asked in a way that was both bold and casual.

"Why do you ask?" Daniel inquired.

"Well, everyone talks about your time up there, but nobody seems to know exactly what happened. Why don't you talk about it?"

Daniel smiled broadly. "I talk about it more than people think, but the answer is so simple that most people think there must be more to it or that there is something I'm not telling them."

"Will you tell me?" the young man asked.

"I will," Daniel replied, and then, pausing momentarily, he took a deep breath before continuing. "I learned to listen to the voice within."

The young man looked confused and disappointed.

"I know people want it to be more sensational and complicated, but it isn't," Daniel said. "It's simple and available to everyone."

A furrow formed in the center of the young man's forehead as he strained to understand. "How did you do it?" he asked now.

"That's the thing, it requires so little doing. You don't have to do anything. Simply spend enough time in silence, and the voice will emerge strong and clear. We are obsessed with doing, but silence teaches us to be, and once we learn to be, whatever we do is infinitely more meaningful and powerful."

"But what did you do with all your time up in the mountains?" the young man pressed, still struggling to grasp what Daniel was saying.

"I would sit in the classroom of silence for four, five, six hours at a time," Daniel explained. "I sat quietly in the cave. I walked for hours each day in silence. And I sat by the lake where the only noise was the soothing sounds of nature."

"What else?" the young man asked, still not satisfied.

"I learned to enjoy silence."

The young man kept asking the same question over and over, hoping for a different answer.

"But there must be more to it than that," he said now.

"I understand why you would think that, but there really isn't, and we could talk about it for days and you'd be no closer to understanding it. It is a mystery that needs to be experienced to be comprehended. So, if you really want to understand it, find a quiet place this evening, a place where you can be alone, and sit in the silence. See how long you can stand it. Most people cannot tolerate five minutes at first. I couldn't stand it for three minutes when I first went into the mountains.

"Observe yourself resisting it, wanting to run from it. Pay attention to the hurry in your soul. What happens when you try to be silent? What happens when you try to be still? What happens when you try to be solitary?

"Then tomorrow, return to the silence, and sit there for a few more minutes than you did today. The day after tomorrow, a few more minutes than that. And little by little, everything will become clearer.

"Consider these two questions: When was the last time you felt truly at peace? How often do you have real clarity about the purpose and direction of your life? These are the gifts that silence will lavishly bestow on you: peace and clarity."

The young man thanked Daniel for his time and made his way toward the town square. As he walked away, Daniel wondered if the young man would take to heart what they had discussed and befriend silence.

## 66. A NEW YEARNING

The days grew cooler, and before too long, the mountains were on fire with the colors of the changing leaves. Autumn became winter, and winter became spring. Another summer came and went, and the streetlights came on a few minutes earlier each evening. One season gave way to another in the natural rhythm that governs all things.

Daniel's father looked older, and his mother moved slower. Getting out of the rocking chair some nights, Daniel felt aches in places he hadn't before.

One year gave way to another, and as time passed Daniel felt the seasons of his heart changing too. Toward the end of the following summer, a feeling came upon him that he hadn't known in quite a while. It was longing. It felt awkward and uncomfortable. He had been living in an extended season of contentment. Still, the longing was unmistakable.

A longing for what? He wasn't sure. His heart was being pulled in more than one direction. There was a part of him that wanted to ignore it, but he had come too far to start deceiving himself in such ways again.

He knew what the longing meant: The time for a new chapter of his life was drawing near.

## 67. RESTLESS

Daniel had settled comfortably into a quiet time in his life. These years on the rocking chair had been marked by a deep peace and contentment. But now something wild within him, something he thought he had tamed, was awakening again.

His longing turned to restlessness. He immediately recognized the significance of this stirring in his soul. It was time for a change.

For the first time since he returned from the mountains, Daniel had trouble concentrating. He needed more time between visitors to gather his focus.

On the outside, nothing had changed. On the inside, the shift was seismic. He knew what would happen if he ignored it: He would become impatient and his joy would begin to evaporate, his ability to serve others would diminish, and in no time at all his unaddressed restlessness would manifest as frustration and resentment. His words and actions would become cold and sharp.

Daniel knew restlessness was a gift. He knew it was a wise and experienced guide. He knew his restlessness indicated an unfulfilled need. It wasn't that he felt empty—not even close. It wasn't that he wasn't fulfilled. Still, he sensed he was being called to attend to his own journey, his own growth. He wondered how he would advise himself if he were sitting in the other rocking chair.

Whatever this restlessness was calling him to, whatever it was saying, wherever it would lead him, he knew he needed to go deep into it. He needed silence, solitude, and stillness.

At that moment, the other rocking chair gently creaked. When Daniel opened his eyes, he wasn't sure if the young man had been waiting for five minutes or an hour. They began visiting, and after a couple of minutes, Daniel smiled.

"What made you smile?" the young man asked.

"I think you and I are wrestling with the same question."

The young man didn't know what to say, and Daniel could tell he was perplexed, so he continued. "You have shared many things with me," he said to the young man, "But what is the one question that is burning in your heart?"

"How do I discern if an opportunity is part of my authentic path or a distraction?" the young man asked.

"What do you think you should do?" Daniel volleyed.

"I don't know," the young man said, shaking his head.

"Yes, you do," Daniel reassured him.

"What do you mean?" the young man said, with rising frustration. "If I knew, I wouldn't have traveled seven hundred miles to seek your wisdom and insight."

"You know that the answer is within you."

The young man seemed dejected. His brow furrowed, and he sat shaking his head.

"Don't be discouraged," Daniel said. "Not knowing what to do is uncomfortable. But it's a mistake to choose the cheap comfort of false certainty over enduring satisfaction."

"How do I avoid making that mistake?"

"Get comfortable being uncomfortable. Don't force your timeline on the question."

"What else?" the young man asked.

"Two more things," Daniel replied. "What would your seven-year-old self advise you to do? Think on that as you drive home."

"What's the second?" the young man asked eagerly.

"Many years from now, when you are sitting on your own rocking chair, watching the sunset in the mountains of Asheville, what will you think looking back? What would your future-self advise you to do?

"It is written: 'We all make choices. That's the easy part. The hard thing about choices is living with them. We all have regrets. We have all said and done things that we would do differently if we could go back in time. But we can't. We may have made peace with those choices to some extent, but still, in the quiet hours they haunt us. Make choices that are easy to live with. Make choices you can look back on longingly, like you do upon the best of times with the best of friends. When you have a decision to make, consult your future self. Imagine yourself twenty years from now, looking back on this moment, and honor what your future self advises you to do.'"

The young man looked dissatisfied. "I guess I had hoped for a different experience here," he said to Daniel with disappointment in his heart.

"That's okay," Daniel responded. "There are many ways to look at this experience. It may not make sense today, but at some point in your journey it will."

"I was really hoping that you'd have the answer," the young man persisted.

"You can spend the rest of your life looking to other people for answers to questions they cannot give you, or you can learn to seek the counsel of your own heart. Other people will lead you astray, but your heart never will. Follow your heart—it knows the way."

It wasn't what the young man wanted to hear, but Daniel knew deep in his heart that he had served him well.

Watching him walk away, Daniel whispered a prayer. It was a prayer of hope and encouragement. He knew that amazing possibilities lay before the young man, and he hoped his young heart had the courage to pursue them.

The young man got into his car, and as he drove out of town, he suddenly wondered, "How did Daniel know I was from Asheville?"

Daniel wondered what his own seven-year-old self would advise him to do now, what his future self would encourage him to do, and how much longer it would be before he saw clearly what was next for him.

## 68. THE NOTE

The sun was setting behind the mountains as Daniel made his way into the house that evening. For the first time in his life, he felt his age. He knew he wasn't old, but he also knew that this feeling was a messenger.

He took the jug of lemonade from the refrigerator, sat down at the table, and began to pour a glass. Half of it ended up on the table. Something had caught his eye on the refrigerator door.

It was a note.

*How did it get there?* Daniel wondered. *How long has it been there?* He would have noticed if it had been there at breakfast.

Getting up, he moved curiously toward the refrigerator. Taking the note in his hands, he gaped at it in disbelief.

*Sophia*
*928-377-6141*

The memory of Sophia wistfully flooded his heart. He had met her only once, and briefly, but he had secretly harbored a hope that their paths would cross again.

"Ezra . . ." he whispered ever so faintly, realizing where the note had come from, as he came out of this montage of thoughts.

A moment later, he was at the back door, pulling on a baseball cap. He stepped out the door and made his way across the lawn, down the lane, and across town.

Ezra Abrams was sitting on his front porch.

As Daniel opened the front gate, Ezra said, "It wasn't me," before being asked. Daniel walked toward the porch, and Ezra continued, "You'd better talk to Mrs. Abrams. She's inside."

Daniel made straight for the front door.

"But, Daniel," Ezra interjected, and something in his tone caused Daniel to pause before opening the front door. "Remember, you may be a prophet, but she's a woman, and intuition is part of their feminine genius."

Daniel smiled. "Thank you, old friend."

Leah was sitting on the couch reading. She seemed to be waiting for Daniel, as if she had known he was coming. "I have a story to tell you," she said as he walked into the living room. "Come and sit on the couch."

He sat on the couch facing Leah. She explained how she had met Sophia in the town square the day she had visited Daniel, and that she had asked Sophia for her phone number.

"I told her I would give it to you when the time was right," she finished.

Daniel sat there, breathless. His mind was leaping erratically between the past and the future. He was torn between honoring his past and stepping into his future. Wrestling with his commitment to a life of service and his own deeply personal needs. His head was spinning, he was having trouble focusing, and he wondered if this was how his visitors felt.

Leah knew what he was thinking, but she didn't interrupt.

In time, Daniel would discover that these seemingly divergent realities were not in competition with one another. He would learn to integrate his past, present, and future into one cohesive vision for the rest of his life. But that discovery wasn't going to happen tonight on Leah's couch.

It was at that moment he heard the voice say, "Be patient with all that is unresolved in your heart. Let life finish asking the question before you rush to answer. It is better to respond than to react. Allow the tension to build. Hold the tension for as long as you can, and the path your soul is summoning you to explore will emerge."

Leah got up and went into the kitchen.

"How did you know there would be a right time?" Daniel called out to her a few moments later.

"I'm a woman," she called back. "We women see effortlessly what you men take years to accept."

Daniel smiled knowingly, and then chuckled to himself.

When Leah returned to the living room, she sat on the coffee table directly in front of Daniel. Taking both of his hands in hers, she looked deep into his eyes and said, "It's time, Daniel. It's time."

## 69. A SEASON FOR EVERYTHING

The people continued to flock to see Daniel. Each conversation led him to examine his own life. Whenever he shared his thoughts with a visitor, he considered how fully he was living that truth.

On his daily walk, he continued to explore his restlessness. He was being challenged to consider future possibilities. And he came to the realization that he had closed his heart to the possibility that a woman's love would touch his life again.

For the first time in a long time, his authenticity was being tested. Would he rise to the challenge that he presented to so many people on the rocking chairs each day? Did he have the courage to go wherever his heart led?

The gentle voice within was speaking to him as clearly as ever now. Despite his questions, doubts, hesitancy, and restlessness, the consistent message over the past several weeks had been: "Something wonderful is about to happen!" He believed that. And as he lay down to rest that night, this is what he heard:

> *There is a time for everything*
> *and a season for every activity under the sun.*
> *There is a time to sow and a time to reap*
> *a time to be born and a time to die*
> *a time to plant and a time to uproot*
> *a time to kill and a time to heal*
> *a time to tear down and a time to build up*
> *a time to weep and a time to laugh*
> *a time to mourn and a time to dance*
> *a time to scatter and a time to gather*
> *a time to embrace and a time to refrain from embracing*
> *a time to search and a time to give up*
> *a time to keep and a time to give*
> *a time to tear and a time to mend*
> *a time to be silent and a time to speak*
> *a time to love and a time to hate*
> *a time for war and a time for peace.*

Daniel wondered what it was time for in his life. He smiled at the future, and the future smiled back.